"Did you see that? He's faster than the Devil himself."

"He *is* the Devil himself," came a reply.

Devlin heard the remark, and liked what he heard. He shouted to the crowd, "Tell Tomas, and anyone else who's interested. This city has gone to Hell, thanks to people like him. Well, this Hell has its own devil now, and people are going to start paying for their sins."

Someone from the crowd pushed his way forward. "What makes you think you're going to leave here alive, Devil. You've only got five shots left and there's more people than that between you and the door. You can't kill us all."

Devlin had to be bold. He pointed his gun at the loudmouth. "I'll take that as a threat against my life," he said and pulled the trigger.

PADWOLF PUBLISHING BOOKS BY JOHN L. FRENCH
Here There Be Monsters, a Bianca Jones collection
Monsters Among Us, a Bianca Jones collection
The Devil of Harbor City
Past Sins
Rites Of Passage: a DMA casefile of Agent Karver and Bianca Jones (with Patrick Thomas)
The Grey Monk: Souls on Fire
The Nightmare Strikes
Bad Cop, No Donut (editor)
Mermaids 13 (editor)
Camelot 13 (editor with Patrick Thomas)
Bullets & Brimstone: a Mystic Investigators™ book (with Patrick Thomas) featuring Bianca Jones
From The Shadows: a Mystic Investigators™ book (with Patrick Thomas) featuring the Nightmare

OTHER BOOKS BY JOHN L. FRENCH
The Last Redhead
Paradise Denied
Blood is the Life, a Bianca Jones collection
The Assassins' Ball (with Patrick Thomas)
To Hell in a Fast Car (editor)
With Great Power (editor with Greg Schauer)

THE

DEVIL

OF

HARBOR CITY

[signature: John French]

JOHN L. FRENCH

PADWOLF PULP

PADWOLF PULP
an imprint of
PADWOLF PUBLISHING INC.
WWW.PADWOLF.COM
www.facebook.com/Padwolf

Acknowledgements
The stories in this book first appeared in different form in the pages of various Fading Shadows publications as follows: "Enter the Devil" *Classic Pulp Fiction Stories 19*, December 1996; "The Devil's Price" (published as "Price of the Devil") *Classic Pulp Fiction Stories 20*, January 1997; "The Devil's Rival" (published as "The Devil You Know") *Classic Pulp Fiction Stories 22*, March 1997; "The Devil's Judgment" *Weird Stories 4*, January 1997; "Deal with the Devil" *Double Danger Tales 13*, February 1998; "The Devil's Wake" *Double Danger Tales 14*, March 1998; "Devil's End" *Double Danger Tales 22*, November 1998

All stories are © John L. French as of the year of publication.
Cover art by Patrick Thomas

THE DEVIL OF HARBOR CITY first appeared in magazine format in November 2000 as a Wild Cat Books publication and is © 2000, 2108 by John L. French

All rights reserved. This is a work of fiction. Any resemblance to any person, living or dead, locales or events is purely coincidental. Except for brief passages used in reviews and criticisms, nothing may be reprinted without the written consent of the author and publisher.

The author wishes to thank Tom and Ginger Johnson of Fading Shadows Publications, without whose support and encouragement Frank Devlin would have never been created.

ISBN 10 digit 1-890096-79-2   ISBN 13 digit 978-1-890096-79-3
Printed in the USA First Printing

From leprechauns to Valley St,
For all the stories he told me
This book is dedicated to
the memory of my father
John French Sr.

Thanks, Dad

TABLE OF CONTENTS

Chapter One
Enter the Devil

Officer Frank Devlin had almost finished the first circuit of his beat when he heard his name called. He turned towards the sound and saw a nun standing at the front gate of St. Brendan's School. It was Sister Mary Carol - warden, mother hen, and best friend to every child she had ever taught.

Devlin had not been one of her students. He had moved to Harbor City only a few years ago, when he was accepted as a cadet in the police academy. He first made her acquaintance six months ago, on the second day of walking this particular beat. A shop owner had caught two of her students stealing from his store. Devlin was about to take them both to Juvenile Hall when Mary Carol, alerted by a third student, suddenly appeared to take charge of the situation.

In the ensuing conflict between Church and State, Devlin had allowed himself to be swayed by both the determined look on the nun's face and his own memories of Catholic school. He wisely withdrew, but only after he warned Mary Carol that if she did not settle things then, he would the next day.

"I'll take care of things, Officer Devlin, don't you worry," the nun told him. "Just check back here this time tomorrow. You will see."

Devlin did come back the next day. He found one of the boys sweeping the sidewalk, the other inside the store stocking he shelves. The third boy, the one who had run for the nun's help, was also doing penance. He too was working a broom, chasing the dirt from inside the store. Apparently, Mary Carol had figured out that it had been a three-man operation, and had dispensed justice accordingly.

Since then, pleased with the way Devlin had both yielded to her and maintained his own authority, the good sister had been coming to him whenever there was a problem she could not handle.

Devlin walked over to the schoolyard gates wondering which of her students was in trouble this time.

"Yes, Sister, what's the trouble?"

"Francis, it's Mary, I think I saw someone follow her from school today."

A little lamb, maybe? Devlin thought. Had it been anyone else, he would have said it aloud. Not to Mary Carol, though. She had a good, and surprisingly earthy, sense of humor, but not when it came to her kids.

"Which Mary, Sister?" There were only about a dozen Marys enrolled in St. Brendan's.

"Mary Ellen Morgan, Francis. She lives over in Hillside." Mary Carol pointed east, in a direction that would take Devlin outside his post, not that that mattered to either of them.

"Who did you see following her?"

"Whom did you see, Francis," came the automatic correction. "It was a young man, I don't know his name. He was dressed well, a little too well for this area and time of day. I've seen him around the school for the last few days. I meant to tell you yesterday, but I missed your passing by the school."

Devlin caught the look in the nun's eyes and the catch in her voice. If the man did something to Mary Ellen, something that could have been prevented by yesterday's warning, the guilt would be with her the rest of her days.

"How long ago was this, Sister?"

"Not five minutes, Francis."

"Then I'd best get going, hadn't I? Call the precinct for me, if you'd please, and tell them that I'm going off post and why."

Getting the girl's address from Mary Carol, Devlin set out along the most likely route she would follow home. He walked it slowly, alert for any cries for help or anything amiss. He also looked for any place the type of man who would follow little girls home from school would go once he caught one alone. If he remembered from the last time he had been up here, this part of Hillside had several vacant houses along the girl's way home.

As Devlin approached the first of the vacant houses, he had not yet decided whether it would be better to search them as he passed by, or to continue on in hopes of catching up with the girl or the man following her. It could be that the man was not following her at all, but was simply going her way. There might also be reasons for his following her, although Devlin could not think of any good ones. As a cop, Devlin had come to expect the worse in any given situation. Given the few times he had been disappointed, he decided to check the houses first.

Devlin walked around the first vacant house he came to. No signs of forced entry, all doors and windows secure. He came to the second one. All was right with the front, and so he walked toward the rear. The back door was open. Devlin slowly entered the kitchen. Once inside, he saw that the door to the basement was also ajar. A light came out of the stairwell, one that, thanks to the dirty basement windows, could not be seen from outside.

A sound came up from the basement. It could have that of a small kitten in distress, or a small child. Devlin ignored the adrenaline rush that demanded he rush down into an unknown situation, and instead eased his way past the open basement door and moved carefully down the steps, hoping not to hear a give-away squeak.

Devlin's search for Mary Ellen Morgan ended when he was halfway down the stairs. Looking over the rail, he saw the girl backed into a corner at the far end of the basement. Her jumper was torn, and her blouse ripped, a bit of her cotton undershirt showing through. There was the start of a bruise on her face, but as far as Devlin could tell, that was the extent of her injuries so far.

Devlin recognized the man who had brought her down here. Tommy Johnson, a low level hood with some high end connections. Devlin had heard rumors about Johnson, but there had never been anything solid on which to hold him.

Johnson had the girl trapped. He was taking his time. He had cut off her escape, and now he was slowly removing his clothing, making his intentions clear to his victim. So intent was Johnson on his prey that he failed to hear Devlin come up behind him.

Mary Ellen's eyes widened at Devlin's approach. He drew his nightstick with his right hand while raising a finger of his left to his lips. He waited until Johnson had both arms occupied with taking off his shirt and brought the stick down on his right shoulder and then across his back. Johnson went down and Devlin hit him again to make sure he would stay there.

"Upstairs, to the kitchen. Wait there." Devlin ordered the girl. She ran past Johnson and up the steps. Devlin dragged the unconscious Johnson over to a water pipe and cuffed him to it. He then went upstairs to find the girl as close to the kitchen door as she could get without actually leaving the kitchen.

"Sister Mary Carol sent me. Are you all right, Mary Ellen?"

Mary Ellen visibly relaxed at the mention of the nun's name. She nodded, then added, "He just hit me, and tore my clothes." She held up an end of her torn jumper then reddened when she realized that her underwear was showing through the rip in her blouse.

Devlin smiled at this innocent modesty and offered her his uniform coat to wear, turning his back to her to remove it so as not to duplicate the scene in the basement. As she put it on he asked, "Are you really all right?"

Just old enough to know what the policeman was asking, Mary Ellen blushed again. "Yes, I am."

Leaving Johnson cuffed in the basement, Devlin took the girl out the front porch and down to a call box on the corner. He called in, asking for a wagon. He then called St. Brendan's. Mary Carol answered at the first ring, and promised to be at the house as soon as possible.

The nun was true to her word. She was there in half the time that it had taken Devlin to walk the same distance. He smiled as he watched her hurry up the street, almost running, her black veil flying out behind her.

Once she caught her breath, Mary Carol took immediate charge of the girl. Devlin allowed her to take Mary Ellen home, provided the girl would be available for questions later. He would not, however, allow the nun into the house.

"This one time, Sister, leave the administration of justice to me."

"I'll hold you to that promise, Francis."

The wagon would be late, he had been told. So, after Mary Carol and her charge left, Devlin went back into the house to check on his prisoner. Going down to the basement, he saw that Johnson was conscious.

"Do you know who I am, cop?"

"I know what you're going to be once you get inside. Shorteyes, isn't that what babyrapers are called? How long do you think you'll last inside? A month, maybe two?"

"I'm not going 'inside,' cop. My uncle in Alexander Tomas, that name ring a bell?"

Devlin knew that name. Tomas was one of Harbor City's major crime bosses. "I've heard of him, so what?"

"So, my uncle runs this city. File your charges, they'll be dropped before you change out of your uniform."

Devlin realized that Johnson was right. Despite all the efforts of the police, the gangs ruled in Harbor City. City Hall, the D.A.'s office, even some of the judges were all on the payroll of some gang leader or the other. Tommy Johnson being the nephew of one of them would explain how the pervert had stayed out of jail so long. No doubt he'd beat this charge too. With Mary Carol depending on him for justice, how would he explain that to her.

Of course, she'd lived in Harbor City all her life. She certainly knew how things were. She'd understand that all he could do was lock Johnson up. Once he'd done that, it was up to the courts and out of his hands. Still, Devlin hated the idea of scum like this escaping justice.

"Hey, cop." Johnson interrupted Devlin's thought. Devlin looked down at the handcuffed figure sitting on the floor.

"What was that little girl's name, cop? No matter, I'll find it out from the charge warrant. She was nice. When I get out, I think I'll pay her a visit, some day when you're off duty."

Devlin's nightstick smashed across Johnson's face, cutting his lip and breaking off his front teeth. Both men were surprised at Devlin's action. With difficulty, Devlin stopped himself from landing a second blow.

What am I doing, he asked himself. "Justice," came the reply from the primal part of his brain, "The only justice this piece of crap will ever see. The justice you promised Mary Carol." That made sense. It might cost him his badge, but the good sister and Mary Ellen Morgan would have their justice.

Devlin looked at the man lying at his feet. He felt the weight of the stick in his hands. He saw the fear in Johnson's eyes. Johnson knew what was coming, knew he had uttered one taunt too many.

"Tommy," Devlin said coldly, "It's time to pay for your sins." The beating began. Devlin was brutal and systematic, being careful not to strike Johnson anywhere that might cause him to lose consciousness. He did not stop until Johnson passed out from the pain. Along the way, Devlin made sure to deliver a few blows designed to make sure that his prisoner would never again be capable of molesting anyone, not in the way he liked anyway.

The next day, Devlin walked into the Commissioner's office and stopped at the secretary's desk. The policewoman on duty stopped typing and asked, "May I help you?"

"Officer Devlin to see the Commissioner," he said formally.

"Oh, yes, Officer Devlin, the Chief's been expecting you. Go right in." With a wave she directed him down the corridor to where Harbor City's Police Commissioner waited. He followed her direction and slowly walked down the hallway. He wondered if he would be walking back with his badge.

Coming to the door he knocked softly and entered. The Commissioner looked up from his desk and gestured him forward.

"Police Officer Francis J. Devlin reporting as ordered, sir."

"Thank you for coming, Officer Devlin," the Chief said kindly, "have a seat."

"No thank you, sir, I prefer to stand."

"As you wish, son, they're your feet, but at least relax, you're making me nervous." Devlin assumed the "at ease" position he learned from three years in the military.

The Chief seemed amused at the young officer's formal manner and said with a smile, "Well, if that's the best you can do I suppose we should just get to it."

The Commissioner looked over some papers, then looked up and said, "Tommy Johnson is in the hospital."

"Yes sir, I know, I put him there."

"Which is why we're having this meeting. Tell me, Officer Devlin, did Tommy Johnson resist arrest?"

"No, sir."

"Then why is he in the critical care ward?"

"Commissioner, you know, of course, of Alexander Tomas?"

"As Police Commissioner I would be remiss if I were not aware of one of Harbor City's major crime bosses. Go on, Officer Devlin."

"Well, sir, Tommy Johnson is Tomas's nephew."

"Which is hardly a reason to beat him up."

"It's part of the reason, sir."

The Commissioner leaned back in his chair, and looked up at the young man standing before him. Devlin had been on the force for five years. Up until now he had received nothing but glowing reports about him. Devlin was a good cop who believed in the law that he enforced. The beat he walked was, thanks to Devlin's efforts, one of most quiet in the city. Devlin had been on the Commissioner's unofficial list for eventual promotion to sergeant. Now, of course, things had changed.

The Commissioner woke up that morning to the ringing of his telephone. Before he could finish breakfast, he had spoken to the mayor, three members of the city council and a newspaperman named Smith, who wanted a quote from him before running a story on the savage beating received by young Johnson at the hands of a brutal cop. All the mayor and the councilmen wanted was Devlin's badge.

"You had better explain yourself, officer."

Devlin then told the Commissioner the entire story, from Sister Mary Carol's calling him over to his canceling the wagon and ordering an ambulance for the comatose Johnson.

The Commissioner said nothing after Devlin finished speaking. He was afraid. What Devlin had said frightened him. One of his best cops had just admitted to taking the law in his own hands, had, in fact, broken the law to see that justice was done for a little girl. What scared him even more was that the Commissioner would have done the same thing had he had been the cop in that basement. What scared him the most was what he was about to do.

Things were as bad as Devlin had said. Most of the judges were on the payroll of Alexander Tomas or one of the other shadow lords that secretly ran Harbor City. The District Attorney was an honest man, but most of his assistants were, at best, questionable. The mayor himself had been elected using monies provided by Tomas and the others. The city was almost wide open to crime and corruption.

The only thing that prevented total chaos was an odd quirk in State law. The law that gave Harbor City its charter stated that the Police Commissioner was to be appointed by the State's governor, rather than the mayor of the city. This was to allow Harbor City's top cop to remain independent of the mayor and above the need to play politics to keep his job.

Thanks to this law the Commissioner had managed to keep his department clean. There were, of course, some crooked cops, but they were the exception and not the rule. Still, it was frustrating to him and the whole department to continually arrest gang members only to have assistant district attorneys drop the charges or crooked judges dismiss the cases. Something had to be done, and Devlin was going to be the one to do it.

"Son, I'll give it to you straight. This morning the mayor called me demanding your badge and I've decided to give it to him."

It was what Devlin had expected, still, it hurt to unpin the shield from his uniform coat and lay it on the desk in front of him.

"And when you get home tonight, you may as well hang that uniform in the back of the closet. You won't be needing it anymore."

"Yes, sir. I understand your position. If I may be excused, I'd like to go back to the station house and clean out my locker. I'll have the uniform cleaned and returned to the Quartermaster's."

Expecting to be dismissed, Devlin had half turned and was preparing to leave when the commissioner stopped him.

"Not so fast, son. Let me finish. I told the mayor that I'd give him your badge, and I will. I'll gift wrap it and hand it over personally. I did not promise not to give you another one."

The commissioner reached into his desk drawer and placed a small black wallet on the desk. Devlin picked it up and opened it to find a gold shield. In place of the words "Police Officer" were the words "Detective Sergeant".

"Sir, I don't understand."

"No, I don't suppose you do. Devlin, you are someone this city has needed for sometime, someone who cares more for justice than the letter of the law. You showed me that yesterday when you risked your job and freedom to see that Johnson was punished for his crimes. Are you ready, are you willing to take the next step?"

"What step is that, sir?"

"I need someone to go after the criminals that the Law cannot touch - the gang leaders, the shadow bosses, the protected racketeers - the ones that the crooked lawyers and corrupt politicians have placed beyond the Law's reach. I think you're the one to do it."

"What would you have me do?"

"Whatever it takes to bring them to Justice."

"You mean?" Devlin put his hand on his service revolver.

"If need be, and the need will probably be often. The scum you'll be going after plays rough, and for keeps. You'll have to play just as rough.

"Don't worry about the legal consequences. I've already talked to the D.A. and the senior judge. Both are on our side. The D.A. will stop any attempt to indict you, and if he's not successful, the senior judge will take the case himself and see to it that the charges are dismissed."

"Excuse me, Commissioner, but that sounds like what Tomas and the others are having done right now."

"Damn right it is. This city is ours, and it's time we fought to get it back. So starting today, it's war. Whose side are you on?"

"What if I go too far?"

"There's always that chance. I'm betting both our lives that you know where to draw the line. Because if you cross it, I'll come after you myself."

The commissioner gestured for Devlin to put the gold badge back on the desk. He placed Devlin's old shield beside it.

"Choose. Pick up the tin shield, and tomorrow you'll be back on the beat. I'll deal with the mayor. Pick the other, and we'll get started taking back our city."

Devlin thought for a moment, weighing his choice, gold or silver. Finally, he picked up the wallet with the sergeant's badge in it.

Pacing it in his pocket, he asked, "Well, now, do you want me dressing up as a bat or a spider or something? Or should I just try to blend in with the shadows?"

The commissioner smiled, "Criminals are a superstitious and cowardly lot, but I'd rather them be afraid of a crazy cop with a license to kill."

There was a silence as the chief let his last statement hang in the air. He wanted Devlin to be absolutely sure what he about to take on, and what he would have to do. Finally, Devlin broke the quiet.

"What's my first assignment?"

"You already have one, Devlin. Tomas will be very happy when his buddy the mayor gives him your old badge. He'll feel that you, and I, have been taught a lesson. When he learns that you are still on the force, promoted no less, he'll come after you."

"Then I'll have to let him find me, and the mayor will have one less friend."

Once more the commissioner reached into his drawer. "Here, you'll need this." He handed Devlin a heavy automatic.

"Thank you, sir, but I'll stick with what I know best."

"You may need more than six shots."

"Commissioner, a good cop always has something up his sleeve."

That night Devlin went hunting. He had to stop in four bars before he found what he was looking for.

Dave's Place, in northeast Harbor City just off of Blair Road, looked like any other neighborhood tavern. Its neighbors, however, knew enough to stay away from there. Situated as it was on the border of several gang territories, it was neutral ground, where members of different mobs could meet in safety and make deals, establish treaties, or just enjoy a night out without worrying about trouble. It was not a place for cops.

Devlin knew this, and walked in as if he were a regular. He had been in three other similar establishments that night. Each time he had nursed a watered drink and waited to be recognized. Sooner or later he would run into someone who knew him as a cop, someone who had heard about the beating he had given Tommy Johnson, someone who thought he had been thrown off the force. Dave's Place was the fourth.

When he walked through the door, a few regulars turned to

watch him go up to the bar. Not perceiving any threat, they turned back to their own business. Devlin ordered a whisky and soda, and dropped a bill on the bar to pay for it.

"Devlin!" He had been halfway finished his drink when someone called his name. He turned toward the voice. The speaker was a young man, vaguely familiar to Devlin, but the cop did not recognize him.

"Yes, can I do something for you?"

"You certainly can, Officer Devlin." This last was shouted loud enough for the whole room to hear. Within minutes everyone was whispering "cop" and pointing in his direction. A few quietly checked their guns.

"I'm sorry," said Devlin's new friend, "It's *Mr.* Devlin now, isn't it? I understand you got thrown off the force today."

"Actually," Devlin said softly, "It's *Sergeant* Devlin." Devlin pulled back his coat to display his new shield.

"And you are?"

"Bobby Johnson, and you're the cop who put my brother in the hospital."

Devlin's smile both acknowledged the fact and indicated that he was proud to have done so. As he smiled, he glanced around him. They had an audience. Good, he wanted one.

"I thought they fired cops who beat up defenseless citizens?"

"They do, Johnson, we only get promoted when we beat up perverts like your brother.

"You know, Johnson, I should have recognized you. There is a family resemblance. How far does it go? Do you like little girls too?"

There was an audible gasp from the tavern patrons. The Johnson brothers were known to be related to Alexander Tomas. His reputation protected them from any kind of a challenge. Bobby Johnson had heard the reaction. He knew he had to respond to the taunt. He also knew he could count on the crowd's support.

But before he could answer the cop and then order that he be thrown out of the bar and beaten the way his brother had been,

Devlin continued.

"You know, Johnson, you probably don't take after your brother at all. From the looks of you, you probably like little boys."

There was only one response to this, and Johnson made it. Devlin's hands were still on the bar when Johnson went for the pistol stuck in his belt. Devlin waited for him to clear his coat when he drew his revolver and shot Johnson in the chest, killing him. He then turned and covered the crowd.

"Anyone else?"

There was, for the first time ever in Dave's Place, absolute silence. Finally, someone in the back spoke.

"Did you see that? He's faster than the Devil himself."

"He *is* the Devil himself," came a reply.

Devlin heard the remark, and liked what he heard. He shouted to the crowd, "Tell Tomas, and anyone else who's interested. This city has gone to Hell, thanks to people like him. Well, this Hell has its own devil now, and people are going to start paying for their sins."

Someone from the crowd pushed his way forward. "What makes you think you're going to leave here alive, Devil. You've only got five shots left and there's more people than that between you and the door. You can't kill us all."

Devlin had to be bold. He pointed his gun at the loudmouth. "I'll take that as a threat against my life," he said and pulled the trigger. Loudmouth's head flew back, a hole where his left eye once was.

"As I said before, anyone else? No, then I'll be leaving now. Do what you want with your friends, call the cops even. I'm sure they'd be glad to search this place for evidence."

The crowd parted, and Devlin quickly left the bar.

IV

The next morning, Devlin was again in the Commissioner's office. He explained how and why he had killed Bobby Johnson, and then told the chief of his killing of the unarmed man.

"You had no choice, son," the Commissioner said after some thought. "He did represent a threat to your life, using the crowd as his weapon. If you hadn't acted as quickly as you did, that mob would have torn you apart."

"A court won't look at it like that, neither will Internal Affairs. That loudmouth didn't have a weapon, and I shot him done in front of a roomful of witnesses."

"That would be true, if it ever comes to court." The Commissioner picked up a pile of papers from his desk. "These are last night's crime reports. Nothing about any killings at Dave's Place. No reports of the finding of the bodies of Johnson or the other one. It's as you said. No one there wants to have the police poking around for evidence. My guess, the two men you killed last night are feeding the animals at some farm upstate.

"So what's your next move?" the Commissioner asked, motioning Devlin to sit now that his official report was finished.

"That depends on Tomas. So far I've killed one member of his family, crippled another and openly defied him. He has to act or the other gangs will see it as weakness and try to move into his territory. I suspect he'll try to kill me."

"And I suspect you're right. How are you going to deal with that?"

"I'm going to give him every opportunity to do so."

Despite the lack of any official report, the two deaths were soon made known to Alexander Tomas. Within the hour of Devlin's departure from the bar, no less than five people had called the crime boss to tell him of the humiliation and killing of his nephew and the challenge made by the Devil. Tomas began making plans to meet that challenge.

V

In the back room of an old warehouse, two men sat quietly, waiting for the man who had brought their drinks to finish serving. He filled their glasses, determined that there was nothing else either of them wanted at that time and turned to go. As he left the room, the sounds of a lively casino came through the opened door.

The younger man took a sip of his beer, testing its quality. Finding it to his taste, he took a bigger drink, emptying a third of the glass.

"It was nice of Lombardi to give us this place to meet."

The older man took a small sip from his wineglass before answering. "Lombardi's being nice has nothing to do with it, Alexander. He owes me several favors. This is just a small payment towards them."

"You're big on favors, aren't you, Louis?"

"They are a type of currency, a hold over another person. Each favor I do creates an obligation on the other's part. When I need something done that would be difficult for my organization to accomplish, it is easier, and safer, to turn to someone obliged to me than to hire someone to do the job."

"Cheaper, too, I suppose."

The older man nodded an agreement, although as a rule he did not concern himself with the cost of things. To him, it was the result that counted, not the means or the cost.

The older man was Louis Martinelli, one of the shadow lords than ruled Harbor City. His criminal organization was small, the smallest of the five main leading gangs that had divided the city among them. Martinelli preferred it that way. He was less of a threat to the other bosses, and less of a target to the police.

Martinelli's host for the evening was Alexander Tomas. Tomas had asked for the meeting, and it was agreed that the two would meet in Lombardi's casino, this week located in the warehouse.

"Louis, I've asked you here to discuss what should be done about that cop."

"What cop is that?"

"Devlin, the cop who killed Robert, and put Tommy in the hospital."

"Ignore him."

"How can you say that, you of all people. This man killed family, I can't ignore that."

Martinelli took another small sip of wine. "I understand vendetta. I also understand what the Police Commissioner may be trying to do. Kill this man now, and you have a dead hero, a martyr around whom the Commissioner can rally his men and the city. Attack him and fail to kill him, and you have created an even bigger hero. No, now is not the time."

Tomas drained his glass, "What then, I'm supposed to wait, for what?"

"For this 'Devil' to try and fail to bring his justice to this city. He will make a few arrests, possibly kill a few more people, then he'll make a mistake, or become discouraged when his efforts fail to produce results. Then you avenge your family."

"And in the meantime, Lombardi, Peterson and Pratt see me as a weak sister, someone who won't stand up for his own. They'll try to take advantage. I should let them?"

"I will talk to them, if you like."

"What I like, Louis, is to see that cop dead."

"If you had already decided, why ask me here? For my blessing? It is a serious thing to murder a police officer. I cannot go along with it."

"If not your blessing, Louis, than how about lending me Nicholas? He could do the job, and we'd be done with this Devil business before it becomes a problem."

Martinelli considered this. "No, I think not, Alexander. I have no wish to become involved in this matter at all, not in your way. Do what you must. I will not hinder you, but I will not help either."

Both men finished their drinks in silence. Martinelli was the first to leave. Tomas waited a proper interval and also left. The next morning he told his men that the man who killed Frank Devlin would receive ten thousand dollars and a favored place in the Tomas organization.

Buddy Williams was the first man to try to collect the bounty on the Devil. Buddy had been in Dave's Place the night that Devlin had killed the two men. He had known both Bobby and Tommy, and hadn't liked either of them very much. The brothers had owed their place in the gang to the fact that their uncle ran it. That was not unusual. Most of the gang leaders made places for family. However, neither of the two boys would let anyone forget their relationship with the boss. It was always "Uncle Alex this, Uncle Alex that." Buddy was glad that the Devil had killed Bobby and crippled that creep Tommy. That wouldn't stop him from hunting the man who had taken them down.

Buddy decided to look for Devlin in the places cops hung out. He tried the coffee shops where detectives on the day shift usually met for breakfast. Then he tried the lunchrooms. He was parked outside police headquarters thinking of places where single cops might go to eat dinner when Devlin walked by his car and started down the street.

Buddy quickly got out of his car and followed the detective at what he thought was a discrete distance. When Devlin crossed the street, Buddy wisely stayed on his side. He did not want to make the cop suspicious. When Devlin stopped to admire something in a shop window, Buddy did likewise. Buddy was enjoying this hunt, and he was sure that his prey did not suspect a thing.

After he had lead Buddy on a half a mile walk, Devlin suddenly turned from the main thoroughfare and went down a side street.

Going home, thought Buddy. *It's about time.*

Buddy crossed over and went down the street just in time to catch sight of Devlin again turn down a smaller street, an alley actually.

"Time to earn that ten thou," Buddy said to himself, and moved his pistol from his pocket to this belt. As soon as he had Devlin alone he'd draw and put one right in the detective's back.

Buddy followed Devlin down the alley and was more than halfway into it when he realized that not only had he lost sight of the cop, but that in front of him was a brick wall. The alley was a dead-end.

"Were you looking for me, Buddy?"

The voice came from behind him. Buddy turned to see the Devil climbing the outside steps of a basement stairwell.

For a brief moment, a very brief moment, Buddy thought about drawing down on the Devil. Then he remembered how quickly the Devil had gunned down Bobby. He slowly moved his hands away from his sides.

"You spotted me," he said with resignation.

"Cops have been spotting you since breakfast, Buddy. Our only question was what you wanted. My guess is that you're after the ten thousand Tomas thinks I'm worth."

"You know about that?" Buddy seemed surprised.

"It's my town. It's my business to know." The Commissioner's informants had known about the bounty ten minutes after it was offered. The Commissioner knew about it five minutes after that. Devlin did not see the need to let Buddy in on the trick.

"Are you going to try to collect, Buddy?" Devlin's arms hung loose. He waited for Buddy to make his move.

Now that Buddy was face to face with the Devil, ten thousand did not seem to be all that much money. He raised his hands to his shoulders.

"Not me, Devil, er, Sergeant Devlin. I was just trying to find you to, to warn you about it. You had no choice but to drop the Johnson boys, it ain't fair that you not be warned. I just wanted to make sure that, that nobody saw me doing it, that's all."

"I appreciate that, Buddy, I really do. And the fact that I already knew about it doesn't make any difference. If you ever need a favor, just ask and it's yours."

Devlin turned and started to walk out of the alley, his back to Buddy.

Thinking, *I don't believe he fell for it*, Buddy quickly drew his pistol and took aim. *At this distance and with that target, I can't miss.*

That was Buddy Williams's last thought. As Buddy was drawing, Devlin turned. His revolver was already in his hand. He fired twice, the first bullet shattering Buddy's forehead, the second hitting his chest, the impact knocking him to the alley floor.

Devlin walked over to the body, his revolver ready in case a third shot was needed. "I don't believe you fell for that, Buddy," he said, as he felt for the pulse he knew wouldn't be there. Devlin stood up and looked at the corpse for a moment. Then he left to find a callbox, wondering just how many more bodies he would have to leave in an alley before this was all over.

In the next week, there were three more attempts on Devlin's life. The first would-be killer decided that the Devil should be killed in his own home. He called one of Tomas's contacts inside the police department for Devlin's address. The contact, who had already been discovered and turned by Internal Affairs, gave the gunman the address of an apartment on the eastside. The gunman spent fifteen minutes picking the lock, then crept into the bedroom and fired four shots into a lifelike dummy lying on the bed. Then Devlin stepped out of the closet on the other side of the room.

The gunman turned as Devlin cleared his throat. He raised his automatic to try to correct his mistake but the Devil fired first. The gunman collapsed across the dummy on the bed.

The second attempt came as Devlin was leaving police headquarters. A sniper had set himself up on the roof across the street. Excited by the prospect of a promotion and ten thousand dollars, the sniper fired too quickly, and his shot went wide, striking the brick just above Devlin's head. Devlin's return shot also missed, but the quick response startled the sniper. He lost his balance and smashed into the sidewalk below.

The third man to go after the bounty was less subtle. He was walking down the street when he saw Devlin go into a neighborhood bar. He hurriedly drew his gun and crossed over. He rushed into the bar after Devlin, intending to empty his clip at the detective and then leave before anyone had time to react.

The gunman pushed open the door, automatic in hand. He

heard the cry, "Gun!" as seventeen revolvers were fired in his direction. He died not knowing that the bar was a favorite after-hours spot for off-duty police officers.

The legend of the Devil grew.

"Word on the street is that you can't be killed."

"Well, Chief, so far the word is right. What else have your spies heard?"

"Tomas's reputation is shrinking. It gets smaller every day that you stay alive. He'll have to take direct action soon. Which is, I suppose, what you planned all along." Devlin nodded and the chief continued. "Department morale has increased. There seems to be overall feeling that it was past time to start fighting back. It's going to be difficult to keep the men from copying your example. I've put the word out that you're operating with my blessing and under my orders, and that any other independent action will be dealt with harshly. One Devil in this city is enough, I don't need a legion of them.

"Oh yes, have you seen these?"

The commissioner threw several newspapers on the desk. Every one carried a story about the Devil on the front page. The papers controlled by the gangs expressed outrage over "vigilante justice" and demanded Devlin's arrest and imprisonment. The reform papers were hailing the Devil has a hero, and calling for full public support. All of the papers were using the Devil's every exploit to sell extra editions.

"Seems like you're a hero, son."

"Until I'm shot down in the street, then I'm just another dead cop. Speaking of which, we do have someone watching the rooftops now, don't we?"

The Commissioner nodded and Devlin continued. "How's the mayor taking this?"

"Our dear mayor does not know what to do. My sources in City Hall tell me that Tomas calls every day demanding action, and threatening to withdraw his support if you're not stopped. On the other hand, the public sees you as more of an avenging angel than a devil, and if the mayor comes out against you, well, elections are coming up, so you should be safe until then."

"Safe from the mayor, which means all I have to worry about is Tomas and his boys. The other gangs should leave me alone until I finish with him. The more damage I do to him the better for them."

"And when do you think you'll be finished with Tomas," asked the chief.

"I'm making my move tonight."

That night found Devlin back in Dave's Place. Like his last visit, few took notice of him when he first walked into the tavern. Eventually someone recognized him, and whispers of "The Devil" began to circulate. Soon all eyes were on him as he stood with his back to the crowd, watching it in the mirror behind the bar. Finishing his drink, he turned and faced the tavern's patrons. No one met his gaze. No one tried to collect the reward.

"I don't see any of my good friend Alex's men here tonight," he said to the crowd. "Of course, I don't suppose he has many men left after the week he's had. Well, I would appreciate one of you telling Mr. Tomas that I was asking about him. Tell him that I look forward to meeting him personally. It's time we settled our differences man to man, if he's up to it that is." There were no loudmouths this time, and Devlin left unmolested.

Like the last time, Tomas received the challenge with the hour of Devlin's departure. The Devil had given him no choice. He now had to deal with him personally. To do otherwise was to risk being labeled a coward by the whole underworld. If that happened, his reputation would be destroyed, his men would defect, and he would soon be as dead as he was going to make Devlin.

Devlin made the necessary preparations. As he had told the commissioner when this whole thing started, he always had a trick or two up his sleeve. Still, he did not expect it to end as it did.

Devlin has finished testifying in Criminal Court against a man he had arrested for armed robbery several months back. As he stepped from the courtroom into the hallway, it was unusually empty. There were no lawyers consulting with clients. There were no court clerks running errands for judges. There were no lost jurors looking for their courtrooms. He was alone.

He was not alone very long. At one end of the courtroom appeared three men, each with their hands under their coats, ready to draw their weapons if needed. Devlin turned around. At the other end appeared two more men. One of them had his gun drawn. Devlin recognized him at once.

"Alex, good to see you. I see you got my invitation."

"You're in a good mood for someone about to die, Mr. Devil."

"That's Mr. *Devlin*, Alex, and you don't mean to say that you're going to shoot me down right here."

"Why not. There's no one around, and I've got four witnesses who will swear that you drew first and I had to defend myself."

"Seems fair. Will I get a chance to draw, or will you take care of that later?"

"Later, I th..." As Tomas spoke his last words, Devlin jerked his left arm. Two shots rang out from the derringer that dropped into Devlin's hand. Tomas and the man beside him fell.

As he fired, the Devil dropped to the floor. The men at the other end of the hall had seen what had happened. They soon had their weapons out and were taking aim at Devlin. With his right hand, Devlin drew his revolver just as the men began to shoot.

Tomas's men had been taken by surprise. Their shots were hasty and their aim was poor. Devlin had been planning his actions since the trap was sprung. His aim was better. He had one live round left when the last man fell.

Devlin stood and turned so that with a quick glance to either side he could watch both ends of the hall. He was looking for movement on the part of any of the fallen men. He heard a moan coming from the end where Tomas lay.

It was not the gang boss. No one could have survived that head wound. The moans were coming from the man lying beside him. Covering the wounded man with his handgun, Devlin went to him.

"Go ahead, Devil, finish me. Send me to Hell."

"I don't think so. You're going to live to tell the tale. This is my town, and I'm taking it back. And Heaven help anyone who stands against the Devil."

Chapter Two
The Devil's Price

It was a pleasant spring day, the first real day of spring after an all too hard winter. In this quiet suburb of Harbor City, children were riding their bikes in the street. Their fathers watched them and talked about the upcoming baseball season. The Harbor City Crabs had made some good trades, and everyone was thinking pennant for the first time in the club's history.

While the children rode and the fathers talked, the mothers sat on their front porches. They discussed vacation plans and traded gardening tips. Some were looking forward to the end of school while the others saw the beginning of their children's vacation as the end of theirs.

In the distance could be heard the roaring of two engines. As the noise got louder and closer, the fathers pulled their children off their bikes and on to the sidewalk. The roaring got louder still and soon two cars came racing down the boulevard. Both were large black sedans. The lead car's back window was shattered and a man was leaning out of it firing a gun at the car behind. The occupants of the second car were firing back, heedless of where any stray bullets may fly.

A child fell, then another. A third bullet struck a father who had been shielding his daughter. Mothers gathered the surviving children into their homes for safety.

The driver of the first car, bent over his wheel, was still desperately trying to elude his faster pursuer. Finally, a lucky shot struck the front tire of the fleeing auto. Its driver lost control. With sparks flying from where the rim met the pavement, the car swerved up on to the sidewalk, rode over a freshly cut lawn and crashed into a front porch where just minutes before housewives sat watching their children at play.

The second car sped off, leaving only spent shell casings on the pavement behind it. When the police finally arrived on Walker Boulevard, it was too late to do anything but count the dead.

That evening, a man set out to dine alone. His companion for the evening had a cold. At least that was what she had told him. Instead, he suspected that she had received an offer more inviting than dining with him. *No matter*, he thought, *I was looking to get out of the relationship anyway. Better that she end it.* With the evening free, he decided to treat himself to a meal at one of Harbor City's premiere restaurants, one he could not have afforded if he were to take a guest.

He decided on the Shot Tower, which featured the finest German cuisine in the city. Not having a reservation, and anticipating a wait, he stopped a newsboy selling the late edition of the Globe. The front page was full of the latest news concerning the massacre on Walker Boulevard, which he first read about in the afternoon edition of the Post.

The paper under his arm, the man walked into the Shot Tower and approached the maitre d'.

"Table for one, please."

The host appeared startled for a moment. "You're here alone?"

Of course I'm dining alone, the man thought, *that's why I want a table for one.* To the maitre d' he said, "Yes, my date had a cold." Then he wondered why he had felt compelled to explain himself. To cover his feeling like a fool, he asked harshly, "Is that a problem?"

"Oh, no sir." The maitre d's attitude was suddenly one of respect. He looked around the dining room. "We have nothing suitable right now, Sir. Would it be possible for you to wait in the lounge? I'll have a table cleared and ready as soon as possible."

"Of course," the man said, thinking that he should "get tough" more often. "Do you need my name?"

The maitre d' chuckled as if he had just been told a very funny joke. "Oh no, sir, I'll remember." He led his guest into the lounge and called the bartender over to take his drink order. Then he went straight for the telephone.

"Barney, it's Frankie," the restaurant host said after making his connection, "Get your boss on the phone." Frankie waited for a minute, then said, "Mr. Kruger, this is Frankie Bloom. Just thought you'd like to know that Tony Peterson just walked in. That's right, Peterson. I've got him in the lounge now. I'm waiting for a corner table to open up before seating him. Yes, sir, he's alone – no bodyguards, no guests, nobody. You're never going to have a better chance than tonight."

Fifteen minutes later the man recognized as Tony Peterson was seated at one of the best tables in the restaurant. It was in a corner, far from the kitchen, next to a window. The man was able to watch the passersby as he ate.

Maybe Donna will walk by and I'll see who she prefers over me. And she'll see what she's missing tonight. He had forgotten that his original plans had not included the Shot Tower.

He had finished his soup. The busser had cleared the bowl and the waiter was bringing his entrée when a sedan pulled up outside. A man with a dark overcoat over his shoulders got out of the back seat. He had a hat pulled down over his eyes and his hands and arms inside the coat. He walked up to the window. Seeing Tony Peterson inside, the man brought his hands up. He was holding a shotgun.

The first blast shattered the window. The second struck the target in his chest. The third was directed upwards into the ceiling, just to discourage any would-be heroes or witnesses. The final blast was unnecessary, but was again fired into the chest of a man everyone thought was Tony Peterson.

The gunman hurriedly got back into the car. It sped away to

tell Enoch Kruger that he had one less rival to contend with.

The two morning papers carried the news that Harbor City gang boss Tony Peterson had been gunned down while dining at the Shot Tower. Later editions carried a correction. It had not been Peterson, but rather Tony Chambers, someone who just happened to bear an unfortunate resemblance to him. Police were investigating the murder, but had no leads at present.

"Table for one, please. I have a reservation."

"Yes, sir, and the name is...?"

"Devlin, Frank Devlin."

If Nicholas, the maitre d' of Martinelli's Restaurant, recognized the name of Harbor City's most notorious police detective he gave no indication of it. After all, was he not in charge of the dining room of the best restaurant in Harbor City's Little Italy, which made it the best restaurant in all of the city. He considered himself the equal, if not the better, of the man who stood before him. True, this police officer had killed ten men, with the Police Commissioner's approval no less. He, on the other hand, had killed more men than that, and the Police Commissioner knew nothing about it.

"Devlin, Devlin, ah yes, here it is, Devlin. Come with me, please."

Nicholas escorted Devlin to a small table in the back of the restaurant. Unasked, a waiter brought Devlin a glass of wine. Devlin sipped it while pretending to study the menu. Within minutes, the maitre d' returned.

"Sergeant Devlin." There was a respect in the man's voice now, and Devlin noted the use of his rank.

"Yes?"

"Mr. Martinelli wishes to invite you to dine with him in his private dining room."

"And I would be happy to accept his invitation. Lead on."

Leaving his glass, Devlin followed the man through a door further in the back. There he found a smaller version of the outer restaurant, with only a few tables, only one of which was set for dinner. The man seated at the table was the one Devlin had come to see.

Devlin nodded his thanks to Nicholas and addressed his host. "Mr. Martinelli, it was nice of you to invite me to share your meal."

"Which you no doubt knew I would once I saw your name on the reservation list. I asked Nicholas to let me know as soon as you arrived."

To the waiting man, Martinelli said, "Thank you, Nicholas, you may tell them to start serving now." He waited until the maitre d' had left and addressed the detective, gesturing for him to sit down.

"And now, Sergeant Devlin, what brings the Devil to my restaurant?"

"I think, Mr. Martinelli, that you know why I am here. It is because of this."

Devlin handed his host some newspaper clipping. The first detailed the chase which had ended in five deaths, the second the killing at the Shot Tower.

"A man shot dead in a restaurant, just because he looked like a gangster. A woman crushed by a car which smashed into her front porch, a man crippled for life. Two children dead on the sidewalk, killed by stray bullets."

"And the driver and passenger of the car, let us not forget them, Sergeant Devlin."

"Their kind are always on my mind."

The conversation paused while waiters brought the food. After they were served and again left alone, Martinelli continued.

"You do not mind if we talk and eat at the same time? Or are you the noble type who refuses to eat with his enemy?"

"If you were my enemy I would not be still sitting at your table. No, I've come to ask you to deliver a message to your fellow mob bosses."

"Fellow mob bosses? Sergeant Devlin, surely you don't believe the lies they print about me in the papers?"

"Mr. Martinelli, let's not kid each other. You run Little Italy as your own small kingdom. Nothing happens inside its borders that you are not aware of. You control the gambling, loan sharking, and other rackets. Your companies supply the local businesses and they pay you to protect them. Anyone who opposes you is quickly dealt with."

"All this, and yet you are here to ask a favor of me? Why?"

Devlin smiled at his host. "As gang leaders go, you're not that bad. You seem to have no ambitions beyond Little Italy. You protect your people, and you look out for everyone in your area. You feather your nest, but you're not greedy. In short, you're a crook, but there are worse ones out there, and they are the ones I'm after."

"That's a strange sort of compliment, Sergeant, but how do the deaths of these people concern me."

"There's a gang war in this city. Up until now, the Commissioner and I have not worried too much about it. The more of your kind that gets sent to Hell the better for the city. And the gang murders give the boys in homicide something to do. Maybe one day they'll actually convict somebody of one of them."

"If there is a gang war in this city, Sergeant, you have only yourself to blame. Your killing of Alexander Tomas upset a delicate balance, and now the other bosses are each trying to seize as much of his territory as possible. There is bound to be some conflict, and with conflict, killing. Each death, of course, requires a response in kind. But I still do not see what you want of me."

"As I said, I'm not all that bothered by your kind killing each other off. It's when their war causes innocent deaths that I become involved. And that's what you're going to help me prevent."

"How?"

"Send a message to your fellow bosses. You've stayed out of this war, so they'll listen to you. These civilians who were killed," Devlin tapped his finger on the newspaper clippings, "I'm going after the ones who did it. Then I'm coming after the ones who ordered it done."

"And how would you find these men? Not many people are willing to talk to the police about such matters, not those who wish to stay healthy."

"We have a few leads on the ones involved in yesterday's killings, and most people are willing to talk if they're assured they won't be identified or have to testify. I'll be looking for information, not witnesses."

"And how will you bring them to trial without witnesses? How will that serve justice?"

"I never said that I'd bring them to trial."

"So they will face the Devil's Justice. Ah, Sergeant, what a price you are paying. To whom has the Devil sold his soul, and how may it be reclaimed? I will deliver your message, though I doubt any good will come of it."

IV

The next day found Devlin at Police Headquarters. The car which had fled Walker Boulevard had been found abandoned several blocks away from the scene of the killings and had been towed to the City impound lot. It was registered to a Mr. Smith who lived at what proved to be an abandoned building. Devlin had asked that a crime lab man be sent to fingerprint it and recover any other evidence from the car. After reporting to the commissioner, Devlin went down to the Lab to see what progress had been made.

He left happy. Prints from the car had been matched to Alan Morse, a member of the Enoch Kruger gang. Kruger controlled the waterfront and part of the West Side. This put him in conflict with both Harry Pratt, who had his tentacles wrapped around organized crime in the business district and Jonas Lombardi, the city's vice lord. With the death of Alexander Tomas, each man saw a chance to expand his empire. Of course, other gang leaders and would-be gang leaders also saw Tomas's death as their own opportunity for expansion. This lead to a war on all fronts, with each mob boss trying to grab as much as he could at the expense of the others.

Devlin did not think Morse was one of the men responsible for the deaths on Walker Boulevard. Morse was more of an errand boy than a gunman. If you needed a message delivered, a payoff picked up, or a witness bribed, Morse was your man. From what Devlin had heard, Morse didn't have the heart for the rough stuff. Still, he was reliable, and could be trusted to do the jobs given him. Like getting a car to use in a gangland hit.

Alan Morse was a happy man. He had just left Lombardi's gambling den on Cheapside St. with money in his pocket. Kruger had paid him his monthly wage, and in just a few hands of cards and a couple rolls of the dice Morse had doubled it. He was feeling lucky, and now he was looking for some place with cheap liquor and cheaper women with the hope that his luck would continue. He was a very happy man.

So he was not expecting to be dragged into a dark alley and thrown against the wall. His head struck the brick and, dazed, he slumped to the ground. Before he could fall, however, he was caught, lifted up, and thrown again, deeper into the alley. He landed against some trashcans, just past the dim lamp that illuminated the end of the cul-de-sac. He laid there, waiting for his assailant to step into the light.

He heard his attacker before seeing him.

"A good place for garbage like you. I should leave you there, but I have questions and you have the answers." The figure approaching him finally stepped under the light.

"The Devil!"

"Very good, Morse," said Frank Devlin. "Ready to pay for your sins?"

"I ain't done nothing, Devil. I'm just a gopher for Kruger." Morse carefully opened his coat. "Look. I ain't even carrying a gun. I never hurt nobody."

"Tell that to the dead from Walker Boulevard. You got the car used in the hit that killed those people." Devlin leaned down and picked Morse up. Once he got the man standing a swift punch in the stomach doubled him over and Morse again collapsed in the garbage.

"Honest, Devlin," said Morse once he could breathe again, "I didn't know why that car was needed. Kruger said get a car, I got a car. Nobody told me nothing past that."

"Which is why you're still alive." Devlin stood over the fallen man and dramatically drew his service revolver. "If you want to stay that way you'll tell me who used the car that night."

"I can't tell you nothing. If it gets out I talked, Kruger'll have me killed."

Devlin pointed the gun at Morse. Slowly he thumbed back the hammer until it clicked. "Well, Morse, somebody has to pay the Devil, and if you want the bill, that's fine with me."

"Wait. It was Frazier and Woods. I gave the keys to them."

That made sense. Eddie Frazier was one of Lombardi's best triggermen, and Tommy Woods one of his better drivers.

"And just where are Tommy and Eddie tonight?"

"I just left them at Lombardi's place. They were losing. Eddie was drinking pretty good."

"Thank you, Morse. That wasn't so bad, was it." Devlin gently released the hammer of his revolver and put the gun away. "Now go away."

"You're letting me go?"

"As long as you don't go back to Lombardi's, you can go anywhere you like, that is, until your boss catches up to you."

Devlin stepped aside and the scared little man ran off into the night. Devlin watched Morse run until he was out of sight and then put him out of his mind. He had more important considerations.

Lombardi's place did not have a name. It was just "Lombardi's." Nor did it have a permanent location. Gambling was illegal in Harbor City, and Lombardi kept his casino in one place just until his informants inside the police department told him that a raid was imminent. Then he would shut down for a time and reopen somewhere else.

Lombardi's place was currently on Cheapside Street, on the second floor of a former cordage company. The owner of the business had had the chance to move to a better location, and had not yet sold the building. In the meantime, he rented the space to Lombardi's frontman.

Like Dave's Place, Lombardi's casino was considered neutral territory. As long as their bosses stayed away, and nobody caused any trouble, Lombardi welcomed everyone, and their money. And as for the other gang leaders, Lombardi ran the squarest game in town, one popular with the city officials on their payrolls. Shooting it up or shutting it down was out of the question. So the casino continued on, the gang war staying safely outside its walls.

Devlin knew about Lombardi's. He didn't care. People will gamble, and at least the gang boss ran a clean game. All Devlin cared about that night was finding his prey.

There was no guard on the outside door. Having a guard standing outside a supposedly empty building was not a mistake Lombardi was apt to make. There were, however, two men standing in front of the freight elevator. Devlin walked past them and toward the stairs.

"Hey, you. You can't go up that way. Employees only."

"That's OK. Think of me as the building inspector." Devlin showed them his shield and at the same time pulled back his coat to display his revolver.

"So you're a cop. You still can't go up unless we get the OK."

Devlin reversed the wallet his shield was in to show his identification. The two men read it and turned pale.

"Now can I go up?"

"Go right up, Sergeant Devlin. We'll let the floor boss know you're here."

"That's not necessary. He'll find out soon enough."

As Devlin went up the back stairway, he wondered if he would not have been wiser to have waited for Frazier and Woods to leave the gambling hall. He could then have taken them without the risks he was about to run. No, he decided, better to have witnesses, both for what he would probably have to do and as a public announcement of what would happen to those who involved innocents and bystanders in their wars.

The stairway led Devlin to a back room, which he could see was devoted to roulette. Devlin did not think his quarries were the roulette kind of gamblers, but he scanned the crowd anyway. The only ones he recognized were a few city officials, one or two judges, and a police lieutenant. The lieutenant would be a patrol officer tomorrow, once the commissioner got Devlin's report.

Devlin went through the other rooms. There was blackjack in one, slot machines in another, poker in a third. Finally, in the room set aside for the dice players, he found what he was looking for.

Woods was at the table, dice in hand. Frazier was watching him. Both seemed to have money riding on the throw. Woods threw an eight, picked up the dice, threw again and made his point. As he picked up his winnings, Devlin stepped to the table.

Standing opposite the two men, Devlin said in a loud voice, "Thomas Woods, Edward Frazier, you are both under arrest for the murders on Walker Boulevard. Step away from the table and keep your hands in sight."

Devlin's announcement silenced the crowd. Half were looking at him, the others were watching Frazier and Woods to see what they were going to do. The smart ones were already backing away.

Both men recognized the Devil. Such was his reputation, neither believed that they would reach the station house alive. Woods made the first move.

Not wanting to start a gun battle in a crowded room, Devlin pushed the heavy craps table into Woods just as he was drawing his gun. The table slammed into the hood and hit the gun he had just pulled from his waistband. The impact caused Woods to pull the trigger and he shot himself in the stomach. He was moaning as he hit the floor.

Devlin still had not drawn his gun. "What about it, Eddie? Your buddy will be dead before the ambulance arrives, if I call one. Want to join him in Hell?"

"You got nothing on me, Devil."

"No? What Tommy just tried to do was as good as a confession," Devlin lied. "A witness puts you at the scene, and I'm betting you weren't even smart enough to get rid of the gun you used."

When Devlin said this, Frazier knew he was trapped. The Devil was right about his gun. He had not gotten rid of it. It was, in fact, in the holster on his belt.

To Frazier, it was die now or burn later. He took the only chance he had. He stepped away from the table. As he did, his hand went to his weapon. It never got there. Devlin, seeing that the room behind Frazier was now clear, beat him to the draw. He fired twice, both shots striking Frazier in the chest. The man fell next to his partner.

The Devil checked the crowd, making sure that none of them showed any signs that they were going to interfere. People were coming in from the other rooms. He looked for the soon to be demoted lieutenant, intending to press him into service, and maybe, just maybe, give him an excuse for being in the casino. He didn't see him. The lieutenant was either hiding in the back, or had slipped out once the shooting started.

"Too bad," Devlin said to no one in particular, "he could have saved his career."

The Devil stepped over to the fallen men. He kicked their guns away from their bodies, sending them under the craps table where only he could get at them. He next checked Frazier. No pulse, no breathing – Kruger would need a new gunman. He turned to Woods, whom he could still hear softly moaning. He checked his wound and found that he may have lied to Frazier. Woods might still make it, if the medics got to him in time.

"You're done, Tommy, unless you tell me what I want to hear," the Devil said to the dying man.

"I'm done anyway, Devil. Rolled boxcars when you hit me

with the table."

"Your choice, Tommy. Who gave the orders for the Walker Boulevard mess? Tell me and I'll call the ambo. If not, well, you can ride in the meat wagon with your buddy."

The Devil waited. He made no move to call for help. "I got the time, Tommy. You don't. What's it going to be?"

Woods wanted to hold out. He knew that if he gave up a name, any name, he's be marked as a stoolie in front of the crowd that was no doubt still gathered. That was a good as a death sentence. Finally, the pain decided for him. Just before he passed out, Woods whispered the name Devlin expected.

V

With Frazier in the morgue and Woods in the hospital ward of the jail, Devlin tuned his attention to the murder at the Shot Tower. This time, there were no witnesses to identify the car used by the killer. This time, however, Devlin didn't need any.

Frankie Bloom had been on his feet for three hours and he needed a break. Since the killing a few nights ago, business at the Shot Tower had never been better. Just like last night, Bloom had started his shift as maitre d' with a full reservation card and a waiting list of over a dozen people. Most of the latter he made wait it in the lounge. The ones smart enough to slip him at least a twenty would suddenly find themselves at a formerly reserved table. Things were going so well that he was thinking of jacking his price up to fifty.

Bloom hated to leave his place, but nature had been calling for the past thirty minutes and would no longer be denied. With a wave he summoned the waiter most likely not to cheat him too much out of his tips and asked him to fill in for a time. Then he headed for the men's room. He did not pay any attention to the man who left the lounge and followed him in.

The restroom was empty except for one man, who left right after Bloom walked in. As the man walked out, he gave a nod to the one who had walked in after Bloom. The second man turned and locked the door behind him. Bloom, intent on his own urgent business, did not notice.

Bloom finished what he had come in to do and was washing his hands when his face was suddenly pushed into the mirror. As his face hit the glass, he heard a crack, and wondered whether it came from the mirror or his cheekbone. He then felt a knee press against his back, and his stomach was pressed tight against the sink.

A hand grabbed a fistful of Bloom's hair and pulled back his head. Then his face was again smashed against the glass. This time he felt the trickle of warm blood run down his cheek. With the right side of his face flat against the surface, Bloom looked in the mirror to his left. As he eyes refocused on the image of what was behind him, all he saw was a very large revolver just inches away from his left ear.

"Now that I have your attention, Frankie, let me introduce myself. I am Sergeant Devlin, Harbor City PD. Nod if you recognize my name."

Between the mirror and the hand holding him against it, Bloom did not have much room to move his head, but he did manage a small nod.

"Good, nod again if you know what they call me and what I'm likely to do if I don't get my way."

Another small nod told the Devil that his reputation was growing.

"Frankie, you remember Tony Chambers, don't you? The guy that looked so much like Anthony Peterson that he got killed for it. Well, somebody here tipped off his killer. I've been watching, and since you've got a phone right at your station, I figure it was you. Am I right?"

Too scared to lie, but not wanting to put himself in for part of a murder, Bloom neither moved nor spoke.

The Devil pulled him back from the mirror. "Talk to me, Frankie, or we'll see if there's a Wonderland behind this looking glass. Who did you call about Chambers?"

Bloom looked at his own bleeding face, then at the man in the mirror behind him. He saw the revolver still pointing at his ear. He gave up the name.

"Kruger, I called Kruger and told him that Peterson was here."

Devlin let go, and Bloom almost struck his chin on the sink. "Go back to gouging the customers, Frankie, and forget we ever had this conversation."

Bloom ran to the door, struggled with the lock, and went out into the restaurant.

Devlin put his gun away, stepped to another sink, bent over and washed his hands. As he did so he thought about what he had just done. Then his thoughts went back to last night and to Morse and Woods. He looked in the mirror. He didn't quite like the man who looked back.

"Who did we sell our soul to?" Devlin asked the Devil. "And was it worth the price?"

"I found out who ordered the hit on Chambers," Devlin told the Commissioner when he reported the next day. "Kruger, who is also responsible for the Walker Boulevard massacre."

"Good job, Frank," the Commissioner sensed that Devlin wasn't finished, and waited for the rest.

"Of course, to get this information I had to terrorize two men, and withhold medical treatment from a third."

"And this bothers you?"

The chief's question was so matter of fact that Devlin was taken aback for a moment. He had expected a reprimand, at the least to be told to take it easy when questioning suspects.

"Yes, sir, it does."

"Good, it's should. I'll start worrying when it doesn't."

The Commissioner folded his hands on the desk in front if him and leaned toward his detective.

"Frank, you knew this was going to be a dirty business when

you took the job. What you did to those men, well, that's part of it. If it's any consolation, all three were instrumental in murder. Frazier directly, Morse and Bloom having set things up. They deserved more than they got. Moreover, as your reputation grows, you'll need to do this less and less. The word will get out as to what you're capable of doing, and soon a threat will be enough to elicit the information you'll need."

Finished with his advice, the Commissioner leaned back in his chair.

"Now then, what's your next step?'"

"Kruger's a thug, the worst of the top five remaining bosses. He holds his organization together with fear, likes to do his own dirty work. It wouldn't surprise me if he had killed Chambers himself."

"And so?"

"And so, I'm going to try to bring him in."

"We don't have enough evidence to charge him, much less convict him."

"I said I'd *try* to bring him in. By now Bloom has warned him I'm on my way. I'm sure that Woods has gotten word to him as well. Like I said, Kruger's a thug. He won't be thinking evidence. He'll be thinking it's him or me."

"Just make damn sure it's him."

A few hours later, Devlin drove up to the Williams St. warehouse that Kruger used as his headquarters. He parked a few blocks away and walked to it, making sure that he wasn't seen. At a distance, he circled the entire building. Satisfied with his reconnaissance, he got back into his car, drove to the front of the warehouse. He parked conspicuously close to the front entrance, making sure that he could be seen from the windows. When he saw a head appear in one of them, and then disappear, he got out of his car.

"Boss," called one of the gunmen Kruger had watching the front. "It's Devlin. He just pulled up and is coming this way."

"You know what to do," came the voice from the back. "Let

him get in, then take him down."

In the darkened warehouse, the two gunmen waited behind packing crates for the door to open and their target to be silhouetted in the doorframe. "I don't see why we can't just shoot him before he walks in," whispered one.

"It's the windows," explained the other, "The way they slant up, you can't aim good. We'd probably miss, and he'd be gone. Don't worry, when he walks through that door, it'll be all over for the Devil."

The two men waited, and waited. Just as the first was saying, "He should have been here by now" there was a shot behind them. They stood and turned around just as Devlin stepped out of Kruger's office.

The Devil had his gun on them, and before they could bring theirs up, he said, "Just lower those cannons easy, boys. I really don't want to kill anyone else this week."

"But how?" asked one as they gently placed their guns on the concrete floor.

Devlin didn't bother to tell them that he had slipped around to the back.

"There ain't no door back here."

Devlin used his revolver to wave the two men towards Kruger's office. *No,* thought the Devil *but there was a ladder and an open second floor window. I got in that way then came down the back stairs.*

"Your boss was as surprised as you were." The Devil said as he motioned the two men into the office. There they saw their boss sprawled across his desk, one hand on the automatic he didn't quite get out of the top drawer.

"Well," said the Devil, "Maybe a little more surprised."

"I want to thank the two of you for coming tonight. I know that it entailed some risk for the both of you. I appreciate the trust you have shown me."

"Only for you, Martinelli," Harry Pratt said as he settled himself behind the table. Jonas Lombardi echoed the sentiment.

"You've stayed out of this war, Louis. No one has any reason to distrust you."

Martinelli's private dining room was much the same as it was when he met with Devlin. This time however, there were five chairs at the table, although only three place settings had been laid.

"Where are Peterson and Kruger?" asked Lombardi, noticing the odd arrangement.

Martinelli paused from pouring the wine to answer. "Mr. Peterson has apparently decided to take a vacation, for health reasons. I believe that his decision came shortly after that premature announcement of his death." Quiet laughter went around the table.

"As for Mr. Kruger," Martinelli lost his smile as his tone grew somber, "I am afraid, gentlemen, that Sergeant Devlin has made good his promise, the one I told you about a few days ago."

"Kruger's dead?"

Martinelli nodded at Pratt's question. "The news had not yet been made public. However, my sources in the police department have advised me that Kruger was killed last night - by the Devil. A contact at the morgue confirmed the arrival of Kruger's body."

Martinelli noticed the waiters bringing in the meal. "Let's enjoy our dinner and think about what this means for the three of us. We can resume our discussion after we've eaten."

Once the table was cleared, and the three men were enjoying an after dinner drink, Martinelli took up where he had left off.

"Gentlemen, the war must stop. It cannot continue without some other innocent becoming involved. Should that happen, any or all of us may wind up paying the Devil's price. That price, as Kruger and Tomas discovered, is much too high."

"We can't just stop," objected Pratt, "there are still some things that have to betaken care of."

"You've both lost men, to each other as well as to Kruger and Peterson. Any one close to either of you? Anyone who cannot easily be replaced?" Lombardi and Pratt both shook their heads no.

"Good, then vendetta is not a problem. That leaves us a question of territory. Harry, I suggest that you assume responsibility for the late Mr. Kruger's area. Jonas, you take over what remains of Mr. Tomas's. The revenue from the two areas is approximately equal."

"What do you get out of this?"

"For myself, Jonas, I get peace of mind. I will not have to worry about being forced to choose sides, nor will I become a target for whoever would have won."

"What about the other gangs, or Peterson if he comes back." Peterson's territory was closest to Pratt's. He was worried that the missing gang boss would object. Martinelli calmed him.

"We will leave Mr. Peterson's territory in the hand of his lieutenants, against the day he finally returns. By the time he does return, the new order will in place. He will not stand against the three of us."

"And what if he doesn't come back?"

"Do you know something we don't, Jonas?" Pratt asked.

Martinelli quickly interrupted. "If Mr. Peterson is in the trunk of a car or other such place, we will know soon enough. We can deal with that problem then."

"And the smaller gangs?"

Martinelli refilled the empty glasses all around. "Let them start the trouble, Jonas. Then let them to go to the Devil."

Chapter Three
The Devil's Rival

Dave Fulton was in a bad mood. His boss Lombardi had had him working all day. A new liquor shipment was coming into the casino, and Lombardi wanted men on hand to make sure it wasn't highjacked.

It's not like the old days, Fulton thought while watching the Canadian liquor being unloaded. Even a year ago, nobody would have even thought of heisting a load of goods from one of the gangs. These days, with that Devil guy running around taking down the bosses, nobody and nothing is safe. Independents think they can walk up and take what they want. There's just no respect anymore.

The delivery trucks were late. Fulton had to help unload. He was held up past the time he had told his girl Bonnie he would pick her up. When Lombardi finally released him, he rushed right over to her apartment. He banged on her door for ten minutes before giving up. Bonnie wasn't the type of girl to sit home on a Saturday night.

Fulton swore. It was bad enough that he had to work all day, now his night was shot to hell. He turned to go. An old woman, one of Bonnie's neighbors, stuck her head out of her own door and called to him. "Young man," she said, quite pleased to be able to pass along her bit of news. "If you're looking for that chippie who lives there, she left about an hour ago."

"Which chippie, the blonde or redhead?" Fulton asked sharply. Bonnie was a bottle blonde, her roommate Betty the redhead. Fulton had tried for her once, and settled for Bonnie.

"Both of them, they both left out of here dressed to shame their mothers."

"Ma'am, you don't happen to know where they went, do you?"

The old woman scowled at him, her gray hair almost touching her eyebrows. "Young man," she said in a correcting voice, *an ex-school teacher,* Fulton thought. "Just what do you think I do all day? I have better things to do than keep track of two girls who are no better than they should be."

"I'm sure you do, Ma'am," Fulton said in a smooth, appeasing voice, knowing full well that was probably all she did. Probably got her thrills thinking about what Bonnie and Betty did on their nights off. He turned to go. "Thank you for help."

"Young man, wait. I think the blonde did say something about going to see somebody's son."

Fulton thought about the places Bonnie and Betty liked to go. "Was it Peterson?" he asked.

"That's who it was, Peter's son. They were going to see him."

Fulton smiled. Bonnie and Betty were going to Peterson's nightclub out on Route 65. He'd grab a cab and meet them there.

Fulton tuned and hurried down the hall, his "Thanks again, Ma'am" flung over his shoulder coming over his shoulder as an afterthought.

Peterson's was on the other side of town, a good thirty-minute ride away. The longer he rode, the madder Fulton became.

"Why Peterson's?" he asked the cabbie, who had been hacking long enough to know that he wasn't expected to answer. "We've passed two other clubs since we've been riding, class joints too. What's wrong with them? Sometimes I think she forgets that she's got a boyfriend. Your girl wouldn't leave you alone on a Saturday night if you came in a little late, would she? No, she wouldn't. It's that Betty's fault, she puts ideas into Bonnie's head."

The rest of the ride was like that, Fulton complaining about his girl, her friend, and why they had to go to Peterson's, clear across town and belonging to a rival gang boss at that. By the time the cabbie pulled into the parking lot, Fulton had worked himself into a very self-justified anger.

He threw a twenty at the driver.

"Wait here," he ordered. "I'll be dragging a blonde out here in a minute or two and we'll go to a swank place, not this dive."

Fulton pushed open the doors and walked past the doorman.

"Forget it," he snarled when asked for the cover. "I'm not staying, just picking up a tramp."

Fulton scanned over crowd. There were too many blondes for him to pick out Bonnie, so he looked for redheads, knowing Betty's henna job would stand out like a beacon. Finally, he saw them at a table in a corner.

They were sitting with two men. Fulton recognized them as two of Peterson's hoods. "Good," he thought, forgetting whose club he was in. "I get to break some heads."

As the doorman he had pushed aside gathered reinforcements, Fulton approached the table. He had a clear view of what was going on. Betty and the guy she was with were locked at the lips in a passionate embrace. Bonnie, thank goodness, was simply watching the show. Then he saw her companion drop his hand into her lap, then on to her thigh. Fulton waited for the slap. It didn't come. The hand disappeared up her dress. Bonnie's only reaction was to giggle and shift to get more comfortable.

Fulton snapped. He had had a long hard day, and he just didn't need this. It was the giggle. Having been with Bonnie, he knew what the giggle meant. She was supposed to giggle only for him. Still, he should have known better. He should have known that he would not be able to get away with gunning down a table full of people in the middle of a crowded nightclub on a Saturday night, not even in Harbor City. He probably did know, but by now he was mad enough that he just didn't care.

Before the doorman, the bouncer and two of Peterson's on-duty men could reach him, Dave Fulton pulled out his piece, an old army .45, and emptied it at the table. The first shot he fired into Bonnie's lap, the next two into her head. He shot her new boyfriend twice in the chest. The shots he had left he shared between Betty and her friend. By the time Peterson's men reached him, his weapon was empty.

In some ways, Fulton got lucky. Had Peterson's been Dave's Place, or some other regular mob bar, he would have simply disappeared minutes after the bouncers grabbed hold of him. His body, and those of his victims, would have been driven far into the country and left in shallow, unmarked graves. It would have been as if he, and they, had never existed. But Peterson's was a more public place. And that's what saved Fulton's life.

It was somewhat of a tradition in Harbor City for the more prominent gang leaders to have their headquarters in a place open to the public at large. Louis Martinelli ran one of the most popular restaurants in Little Italy. Jonas Lombardi ran a casino, which, while illegal, was an open secret and considerably more popular than Martinelli's restaurant. Anthony Peterson, when he was in town, conducted business in his nightclub.

There were reasons for this public accessibility. True, it made it easier for the police to find them, but by being seen at their establishments at least once at night, there were always one or two honest citizens willing to swear that the bosses had been there *all* night, making alibis a lot easier to come by. Also, by putting on a Damon Runyon "gangster with a heart of gold" act, these men made themselves seem less threatening to the public, and that public was then less likely to press the politicians and police to take needed action, or to support them when they did.

So when Dave Fulton emptied his gun into the people sitting at table number four, too many private citizens were present for the normal course of Harbor City gang justice to run its course. Like it or not, the management had to call the cops.

"What have we got?" Detective Sergeant Benjamin Campbell asked the uniformed officer guarding the scene.

"You're not going to believe this, Sergeant."

"Try me." Campbell had been a Harbor City cop for fifteen years, the last eight of them in homicide. He doubted if anything the officer told him could surprise him.

"We got four people dead, the perp standing over the body with the gun in his hand, and three witnesses who say they saw him do the shooting."

Whatever Campbell was going to say next stuck in his throat. A gang involved slaying with enough hard evidence to convict. The beat cop was right, he didn't believe it. Three hours later, after taking statements from the three men who stayed behind to do their civic duty and tell the police everything that they saw, he still didn't believe it. And the next day, after the ballistics lab confirmed that the gun taken from Fulton by the doorman and dutifully turned over to the police was indeed the murder weapon, Sergeant Campbell still didn't believe it. This was Harbor City, after all, and solved murders involving gang members just did not drop into his, or any cop's, lap. And it didn't take long before he was proven right.

Fulton had not been in jail for more than an hour when Jonas Lombardi got the news of his arrest. Lombardi's first reaction was to let his employee, no, ex-employee, rot. You killed for money, for power, for revenge; you did not kill over a woman. Anyone who did not understand that deserved whatever happened to him, even it was the hot seat.

Then common sense prevailed. Fulton had been a member of the Lombardi mob for a long time, he knew a lot about the organization. Looking at a date with the electric chair, Fulton could easily trade this knowledge for a life sentence in an out of state prison.

Lombardi's next thought was to simply kill Fulton. He had men inside the prison who would do the job. One call, and Fulton wouldn't be alive to make bed check. He picked up the phone and was about to dial when he thought better of it.

These were tough times in Harbor City. Thanks to that crazy cop they called the Devil, two gang bosses were dead, and he and the rest were looking over their shoulders. The men were nervous, and loyalties were strained. Now was not the time to kill one of his own.

He would have to spring Fulton. That would show the rest of his men that he'd back them all the way, and should reinforce their loyalty. It would also demonstrate his power to the rest of the gangs.

Lombardi got the word to Fulton. Stay calm, keep your mouth shut, and you'll be okay. Talk, and you'll be dead before the words leave your mouth. Fulton, who had been ready to start dealing for his life, promptly shut up, demanded a lawyer, and waited for his boss to keep his word.

In earlier times, fixing this case would have been a simple matter. A bribe to the judge would get any evidence that could not be explained away excluded. A witness or two gets killed and the others would withdraw or suddenly develop amnesia. That was before Frank Devlin and his special assignment to hunt down and bring to justice those who, by one means or the other, had escaped or were beyond the reach of the law. When Devlin passed sentence there was no appeal. The gangs called him "The Devil," and it was a name well earned.

If anyone killed the witnesses in the Fulton case, he would become Devlin's special prey. And once the killers were brought down, Devlin would go after Fulton, just to send the message that no one could escape justice in Harbor City.

So Lombardi had to use a subtler approach. His casino in the waterfront area was open to all who could find it, and many did. Some of these gamblers won, most lost. Many of those who had lost were still in debt to Lombardi, having signed IOUs at usurious interest rates to cover their losses. Lombardi simply offered to cancel the debts owed by three of these men if they would testify that Fulton had been playing poker with them the night of the shooting.

These men were not gangsters. One was a banker, who could now stop taking money from inactive accounts to pay the interest he owed Lombardi. Another was a grocer, who finally saw college in his child's future. The last was a teacher, who had been about to leave everything in the hopes of escaping Lombardi's clutches. These three men were offered a way out of bondage, and to take it, each took the stand and perjured himself.

Getting rid of the weapon was even easier. Transferred to the custody of the courts on the day the trial started, it disappeared from the evidence locker that same night. When the D.A. was unable to produce the .45 in court the next day, the judge excluded all evidence relating to it.

With no physical evidence to consider, and the identification of the eyewitnesses cast into doubt by three equally respectable citizens, the jury lost no time in bringing in a "not guilty" verdict. The judge quickly set Dave Fulton free.

They threw a party for Dave Fulton when he was finally released from jail. At that party, Lombardi handed him an envelope containing five hundred dollars and a train ticket out of town. He reminded Fulton that his acquittal, based as it was on questionable witnesses and missing evidence, would bring him to the attention of Frank Devlin. Not only that, but some of Peterson's gang would no doubt be looking for revenge. He could probably square things with that gang, especially if their boss stayed out of town. But if Fulton wanted to remain free and alive, he should, with Lombardi's blessing, take the morning train for Florida for a much deserved vacation, far away from the Devil. It was hoped that by the time Fulton returned, Frank Devlin would have forgotten about him.

After the party, Fulton made his way back to his rooms. As he shut his apartment door and turned on the lights, he did not see the figure sitting in the corner chair. The first hint of an uninvited guest that Fulton had was the click of a revolver hammer locking into place. Fulton froze, and without turning around, slowly raised his hands in the air.

"If that's you, Devil, you got nothing on me. The court let me go on the murder charge, and I ain't got a gun."

"Turn around, Fulton," said the man in the chair. "You may as well see it coming, unless you want it in the back."

"I'm telling you, Devlin, I'm not gonna give you any trouble, you want to take me in, take me in and we'll sort this out."

Fulton turned to face his assailant. The man in the chair stood up and stepped out of the shadows. As soon as Fulton saw the face of the man who would kill him, the man opened fire. Six shots later, Dave Fulton lay dead on the floor. The man took a card from his pocket and threw it on Fulton's lifeless body. Then he quickly made his way out of the rooming house, taking care not to be seen by any of the other boarders.

No one in the apartment would have seen the killer. Long time residents of the area, they knew what to do when gunfire started - stay low, keep out of sight, and pray that no stray shots came your way. No one looked out when Dave Fulton was sent to his reward. At least one, however, called the cops.

When the police arrived, the killer was again in the shadows, this time watching the activity from across the street. As the uniformed officers entered the building, the man consulted a notebook he had taken from his pocket.

"That's one," he said to himself as he crossed Dave Fulton's name off a list. "It's going to be a busy night."

By daybreak, four more men lay dead by the killer's hands. Two were murderers who, like Tony Fulton, had been released by the courts for "lack of evidence." They were gunned down in the street. Another of the victims had preyed on young children, some belonging to rich and powerful families. However, his father had been richer and more powerful, and his trial was a mockery. He was found shot to death in his car. The last was a bank robber. The police had interrupted his last heist so he took a woman hostage to aid in his escape. He abused her horribly before leaving her bleeding on the side of the road. She was still in critical condition in County Hospital. When caught, the robber was allowed to plead to simple assault and misdemeanor theft by an Assistant D.A. with mob connections. Like Fulton, the robber had been killed in his own apartment, the police called by neighbors who had heard the shots. Lying next to each of the bodies was a simple pasteboard card bearing the image of a stylized pitchfork, one of the marks of the Devil.

Frank Devlin had planned to spend the day trying to find Anthony Peterson. The gang leader had still not resurfaced following the attempt on his life. Devlin wondered if someone had finally succeeded in killing him or if Peterson was just in hiding. His plans changed when an early morning telephone call summoned him to the Commissioner's office.

Devlin greeted the Commissioner's secretary with his usual cheery "Good Morning!" but instead of receiving a similar greeting in return she said simply, "Go right in, they're expecting you."

Her "they" had Devlin wondering. He and the Commissioner always met in private. The work he did for Harbor City's top cop was best discussed alone. Of course, what that work was public knowledge. He had been written up in the Harbor City newspapers several times. He was the Law's Last Resort. When the justice system failed, The Devil could be counted on to restore the balance. Still, their discussions about his violent crusade against the mobs were not ones that either wanted to trust to the memories of witnesses.

When Devlin entered the office, he saw why the secretary had been upset. Standing to the right and a bit behind the Commissioner's desk was Anton Szold, the head of the Harbor City Police Internal Affairs Unit.

When the current police commissioner was appointed, the plague of corruption that had infected the offices of the mayor, the District Attorney and several judges was beginning to spread to the police. As a vaccine, the Commissioner appointed Anton Szold to head the Internal Affairs Unit. Szold had been a federal prosecutor, whose reputation was such that a national magazine had once tagged him "more honest than God." When political pressure was brought to bear on his office to prosecute what to him was a clearly innocent man, Szold resigned, joined the defense team, and won the man's acquittal.

Szold accepted the Harbor City assignment on several conditions. The first was that he had total control over his investigations. The next was that he hired his own investigators. The last was that he reported not to the Police Commissioner, but rather directly to the District Attorney. The chief readily agreed, and the result was that Harbor City now had the reputation of having the most honest cops in the country.

When Devlin saw Szold standing behind Commissioner, who was sitting almost at attention at his desk, he again assumed the military manner that had marked his first visit to this office.

"Detective Sergeant Frank Devlin reporting as ordered, Sir." Had he been in uniform he would have saluted.

"At ease, Sergeant." The Commissioner matched his formality, with no trace of the humor that he had displayed at their first meeting.

"Sergeant Devlin, you will surrender your service revolver and any other firearm you have on your person to Mr. Szold."

Without comment, Devlin removed his gun from its holster, broke the cylinder, unloaded the weapon and handed it and six cartridges to Szold. Accepting the weapon, Szold checked to make it sure that it was unloaded. He turned to the Commissioner with a questioning glance.

In answer, the chief asked Devlin, "That's it, Sergeant?"

"I did not think to come fully armed. My other weapons are at home."

"Not to worry," Szold's voice was quiet, a chilling whisper that dominated the room, "We'll find them in our search." He handed a paper to Devlin.

To the Commissioner he said, "I'll take this to ballistics." and left the room without another word.

When Szold had left the room, Devlin looked at the paper he had been handed. It was a warrant to search his apartment and car for any and all weapons that may be found there. Without breaking his "at ease" stance he asked, "Sir, what is this about?"

"Sergeant, last night five men were found shot to death. Several things link their deaths. All had been criminals. All had recently been tried for murder or other serious offenses. All were either acquitted or else received an extremely light sentence that put them back on the street. All were killed with a .38 similar to the ones issued the police."

"And that makes me a suspect." It was a statement of fact, not a question. Again, Devlin recalled their first meeting. The Commissioner had told him then, "If you cross the line, I'll come after you myself."

"That makes you a suspect, that, and this." The Chief threw a card on the table. "I have four more just like it. One was found on or near each of the murdered men."

Devlin picked up the card with the image of a pitchfork.

"I'm supposed to be this stupid?"

"No, but you may think you're above the Law, and so you're marking your kills, taking the credit and leaving a warning, like those fellows in the pulps do."

"And what do you think?"

"I'll let you know when Szold calls back. You may as well have a seat, neither of us is going anywhere until he does."

The two spent an uncomfortable seventy minutes. Neither tried to start a conversation. The chief tried to get some of his ever-present paperwork finished. He made little headway, but stayed with it so as not to have to look at the man in front of him, the man he had set loose in the city.

For his part, Devlin stared everywhere but at his boss. For the first time he understood what it was like to be suspect, to weigh everything you had done lately against how the police might interpret it, to realize that your actual guilt or innocence did not matter, that your freedom depended on another's decision.

The telephone's ring startled both men. Devlin was half out of his seat to answer it when he remembered whose office he was in. The Commissioner gave him a half smile and answered the phone.

"Yes, I see, well, I expected as much. What about his apartment? .45 derringer in a sleeve gun, .32 in an ankle holster, throwing knives and what?" The Commissioner looked up at Devlin. "What are you doing with a crossbow?"

"It was my mother's."

The chief decided not to follow through and went back to the phone. "What about another .38? No calling cards or anything like that? Good. I'll expect a copy of your report, Mr. Szold, and, thank you."

The Commissioner hung up the phone and addressed Devlin, "You're off the hook, son. Your gun doesn't match the bullets from the victims, and there's nothing incriminating in your apartment."

"I could have another place that you don't know about."

"Do you?"

"No."

The Commissioner laughed. "I believe you. Not that I thought you had done it the first place, but ..."

Devlin interrupted, "But you had to be sure. I wouldn't expect anything else."

"I'm glad you feel that way. Well. So much for the good news, ready for the bad?" Devlin nodded, and the chief went on. "The papers have already picked up on this story. Tonight's Sun and tomorrow morning's Sentinel and Chronicle will be running stories about the murders. I've seen advance copies. All of them mention you as the likely suspect. Of course, the following editions will carry the fact that you've been cleared, but the damage will have been done."

"Don't."

"Don't what?"

"Don't tell them that I've been cleared. Just say that the investigation is on-going and that you're looking at all possible suspects."

"That will make it look like we think you're guilty."

"And it will let this other Devil think so too. With him off his guard, it may be easier to nab him."

The Commissioner frowned. He clearly did not like the idea. "My thought was to clear you quickly, before the gangs decided to take you down."

"The gangs have always wanted to take me down. They haven't yet."

"That was before. Up until now you've played the game, always giving your targets a fair shot at you. What happened last night changed the rules. Lombardi, Peterson, and Pratt each lost men last night. They'll be scared, and will come at you with guns blazing."

"Let them come, when it's finished there'll be less of them to worry about."

It did not take long. That same evening, after Devlin had finished eating and was walking home from the restaurant, he heard the screech of tires behind him. He turned to see a long black car bearing down on him. There was nowhere to hide. Whoever had seen him and plotted the ambush had planned well. There were no stairwells or alleys in that block to provide cover. The street was well lit, making him a perfect target. If he ran, he would be run down. If he stood his ground, bullets from the death car would find him easily.

It was not in Devlin to run. Instead, he flattened himself against the dark brick of the wall behind him. His first shot was not at the car, but rather upwards, his bullet shattering the street lamp spotlighting him before the car could come into range.

Partially hidden by the dark, the Devil switched his gun to his left hand, squeezed off two quick blasts at the passenger side of the car and dropped to his right. There was a short cry of pain followed by return gunfire. As he had hoped, the shots from the car were wide to the left, the gunmen aiming at the muzzle flash in the darkness.

The sedan sped past him. When it reached the end of the block Devlin expected its driver to turn around for another pass.

Instead, the driver got what he thought was a brilliant idea and suddenly stopped the car and reversed back down the street.

Had Devlin remained where he was, this maneuver would have given the marksmen on the passengers' side a better chance of killing him, as well as protecting the driver from his gunfire. The Devil, however, had sensed what was coming as soon as the car had stopped, and had rushed across the street on an angle toward the oncoming vehicle.

Able to see only out of his rear windshield, and with his vision partly blocked by the man in the back seat, the driver did not see Devlin until he had run up beside him. As he drove backwards past the Devil, he lived only long enough to watch him put a bullet into the chest of the man beside him. Another shot and his own life ended, his blood spattering the gunman in the back seat.

With no one alive in the front seat to control the car, it drifted backwards down the street. As he watched it, Devlin did not know whether to hope for the remaining passenger's survival or not. He was already tired from dodging bullets and Buicks, and not in the mood for another gunfight. On the other hand, a dead gangster could not tell him who had planned this little surprise for him. He truly wanted to return the favor.

Devlin's dilemma was ended as the back door of the car opened and its passenger sprawled out on to street. Watching his foe, Devlin walked slowly toward him, reloading his revolver as he went. Seeing some slight movement, but no threat, Devlin sighed and whispered to himself, "Well, time to play the Devil." In the background there was a crash, and Devlin idly wondered what the sedan had run into.

Devlin came up on the fallen man, noted that his hands were empty of weapons and, unmindful of any injuries, turned him over. The pain brought the gunman back to consciousness. As his eyes focused, all he could see was the barrel of a very large gun and an even larger man behind him.

"Ready to pay for your sins?" The words were soft, filtered through the cotton of his concussion, but the meaning was clear enough. Expecting a gunshot to end his life and send him to hell, the gunman was surprised to hear a question instead.

"Who?"

In his dazed state, the gangster almost said, "He's on first" but recovered in time to understand the question. He focused again on the gun and with this reminder of his mortality gave up the man who had sent him on this ill-fated ambush.

"Pratt." Devlin nodded as the man passed out. He left him there for the ambulance crew to find as he went to see what damage the sedan had caused.

IV

The next day Devlin was again in the Commissioner's office. This time the mood was lighter. The chief's secretary returned Devlin's greeting and directed him to the back with a big smile. The Commissioner, still at his paperwork, simply waved Devlin to his usual seat.

"Busy night last night, son."

"I'm going to have a busier afternoon. I'm paying Pratt a visit to explain why it isn't nice to try to kill policemen."

"Need any help?"

"I shouldn't. Unless he insists otherwise Pratt will still be alive when I leave - scared but alive."

"Good, we don't need you starting another gang war. We need to find a way to jail these mob bosses and make it stick, not just kill them off to be replaced by ones just as bad."

"Then why am I the Devil?"

"To keep them busy until we can jail them, and to make sure there's at least rough justice to balance the scales they've managed to tilt in their favor."

The Commissioner threw a handful of newspaper at Devlin. "More good news. The papers carried the story of the murders, and all of them seem to think that you did it."

Devlin was puzzled. "That's good news?"

"It is if we want your rival's guard down. Anyway, the good news is that if you read between the lines, the Sun and Chronicle approve of what 'you' did. 'Much needed justice, however applied' was my favorite line."

"What about the Sentinel?"

"The Sentinel's controlled by Pratt. The editors, of course, want you suspended at once, tried immediately, and then hung."

Devlin laughed. "I really ought to stop reading that paper, but it has the best comics." Devlin put the papers back on the Chief's desk.

"Any progress on finding my rival?"

"Not much, but there's not much to go on." The Commissioner then threw the question back at Devlin. "What do you think?"

"If it had just been Fulton, I'd say it was payback for the nightclub killings. But taken with the other killings, there are just two possibilities. One is that it's someone from one of the gangs, somebody out to discredit me and even a few scores at the same time."

The Commissioner nodded to show that this had occurred to him as well. Devlin went on. "It could also be another cop, thinking that he's somehow helping me. But why now, and why all five in one night?"

"Maybe he's just trying to catch up, Frank. Or catch you up. You haven't been in the papers that much lately."

"I know, I've been trying to find out where Anthony Peterson's gotten to. It looks like he may have just gone away for his health, but I wanted to make sure. Besides, until last night, no one's tried to kill me for awhile, so there's not been that much to write about."

"So our minor demon, to whom you're a hero, decides that you've been laying down on the job and gives you a hand."

"So how do we catch him?"

"I've got people working on the mob angle. Who benefits by any of these deaths, where they were that night, etc. I'm also quietly checking our coworkers. Each precinct, a squad at a time, is being called out to the range to 'requalify' with their service revolvers. After they've finished, the fired bullets are recovered from the targets and taken to the ballistics lab. If we're lucky, one will match up with the murder bullets. If it does, that will at least narrow it down."

"That will take some time, assuming it is a cop and that he used his service piece."

"We're doing all we can, and we'll just have to wait for results."

"Or until he strikes again."

Unlike his fellow mob bosses, Harry Pratt avoided public scrutiny at all cost. He firmly believed that out of sight was out of mind. He had his headquarters in a suite in an old office building in a less than prosperous part of town. From there, he ran a business that included gambling, loan sharking, prostitution, and the smuggling of unlicensed cigarettes and liquor. Pratt also provided money and influence to the smaller gangs in return for future favors or a cut of the profits. Finally, he controlled what crime there was in Harbor City's business section, running laundry, maintenance, and protection rackets, all the while making sure that any union that was organized soon fell under his control.

Frank Devlin's sole purpose in visiting Harry Pratt was to deliver a message. He did not expect any trouble, but just the same took all his usual precautions. Ankle and sleeve guns in place, his .38 cleaned and loaded, he calmly walked through the door of Pratt's second floor office.

As he walked in, he noticed two men in the waiting room. From the way they watched him when he entered, they seemed to be waiting for him to start trouble. So rather than walk up to the secretary's desk, he stood where he could see them both and announced, "Detective Sergeant Frank Devlin to see Mr. Pratt."

Both men stood at once. Keeping his hands away his body, and before the men could move theirs to the guns on their belts, Devlin said quietly, "You boys that anxious to die?"

Neither man moved. They had heard stories that the Devil could draw his gun faster than a man could blink. Neither wanted to try him, but neither did they want him to kill their boss and put them out of work.

Devlin reassured them. "I'm just here to talk. If there's to be any gunplay, Pratt will have started it. You have the Devil's own word on that."

To the relieved secretary Devlin said, "I'll just go in and see Mr. Pratt now." He walked through the door marked "Private" before anyone could object.

Harry Pratt looked up from his desk when Devlin entered his office. Before he could object to this unexpected visit, Devlin took a seat in front of his desk.

"Hello, Harry."

"Devlin. How'd you get past my boys?"

"Your boys decided that they'd rather be fired than buried. Besides, I promised them that I wouldn't kill you."

"Damned nice of you."

"I thought so. Of course, I'm likely to regard any sudden movements on your part as a threat on my life and have to break my promise. Understand?"

"Understood. Neither of us wants trouble. Now, what do you want?"

"Just a word of warning, Harry. Your men tried to kill me last night." Devlin held up a hand to forestall Pratt's inevitable objection. "I know, anything your boys did last night was done without your knowledge or approval, and if anybody says otherwise it's his word against yours. Right?"

"Damn right. Now you here to arrest me or what?"

"Arrest you for what? If I had hard evidence we wouldn't be having this chat. Like I said, I'm just here to give you a warning." Devlin leaned back in his chair and waited for Pratt to break the silence.

"Well?"

"Well what, Harry?"

"What kind of warning?"

"Harry, the next time somebody, anybody, shoots at me, and your name comes up the way it did last night, I'm going to hunt you down and kill you in self-defense."

"That would be murder, Devlin, you'd never get away with it."

Devlin just smiled at the gang boss. He picked up a copy of the Sentinel that was on Pratt's desk. He flipped it open and looked at the front page. He saw his own face looking back. He folded the paper so that his photo was facing out.

"You'd be past caring, Harry." Devlin handed the paper face up the Pratt. "Besides, who says I wouldn't get away with it. Don't you believe what you print in your own paper?"

Devlin stood up. "Be good or be dead, Harry. I'll see myself out." Devlin walked over to the door. He opened it, then turned back to Pratt.

"By the way, Harry, you might want to pass the message on to Lombardi and Martinelli. Anybody comes gunning for me, someone will pay the Devil. And I don't give a damn which of the three of you it is."

Devlin closed the door behind him. The relieved bodyguards stood up.

"Your boss wants to see you two. He's not in a good mood."

"Do you think he got the message?" The Commissioner asked Devlin once the latter reported in the next day.

"He got it. I gave him it to him straight and hard, and left before he could get the last word."

"What's next for you, son?"

Devlin settled himself on the couch in the office. "It depends, how's the investigation going on your end?"

"Not good," admitted the Commissioner. He picked up a file from his desk. "The whereabouts of all the investigators involved in any of the cases that went sour have been accounted for. The 'requalification' is continuing, but so far none of the recovered bullets match those from the gun your rival's used."

"If he is a cop, he's probably not using his service weapon anyway. Any word from the street?"

The Commissioner smiled. "Plenty, everyone says you did it."

"I could go to ground for awhile," suggested the Devil. "Wait for him to strike again."

The smile on the chief's face quickly faded. "You'd let more people be killed?"

"It might be necessary. We don't have that much to go on now. Besides, whether I'm in town or not, we both know he'll do it again. After all, he got away with it the first time. He committed five murders and I got the blame. What's to stop him?"

"What is stopping him?" wondered the Commissioner aloud. "It's been four days. I'm sure he's got others on his list. Lord knows in this city that list has to be pages long."

"Night shift," Devlin said softly.

"What was that, son?"

Devlin stood up and went over to the Commissioner's desk. "He's working the night shift, five on, two off," he said excitedly. "That's why he hasn't struck again. He can't do his patrol and play the Devil both at the same time."

The Commissioner nodded his agreement. "That's possible. I'll get personnel to make up a list of those officers who were on leave that night."

"And I just got an idea on where he got his second gun."

"You were right, Frank. Good job."

"I would have preferred to be wrong."

"You and me both, son." The Commissioner looked over the latest additions to his file on the vigilante murders. A list of officers who were off on the night of the killings, a second list of officers who had reported losing their weapons and who, after paying a fine and being issued extra duty assignments, had been issued new ones. Just one name appeared on both lists.

"This doesn't mean he's the one," offered Devlin. The Commissioner raised his head from the papers. The look he gave Devlin said that he didn't believe that anymore than the sergeant did.

"I'll turn the results over to Szold," the chief said wearily as he closed the folder.

"Commissioner, I'd prefer that you let me handle things, Szold would go public."

"We're talking about brother cop here, Frank. You sure you can handle it?"

"We're talking about a murderer who happens to wear a badge. He sure as hell isn't my brother."

Brian Douglas had had a long day. He had worked the night shift, then another eight hours on day shift handling telephone complaints. Thank God his forty hours punitive time was almost over.

It was five in the afternoon when Douglas finally made his way back to his rooms. As he shut his apartment door and turned on the lights, the first thing he saw was a figure sitting in a corner chair.

The man in the chair stood up to greet him. "Officer Douglas, I'm Frank Devlin."

"The Devil!"

"The one and only. Douglas, I know what you've been doing, and it stops tonight."

"Listen, Frank …"

"Sergeant Devlin, to you, Officer - or Devil, if you prefer."

"Sergeant, I'm just trying to help."

The Devil held up a .38 police special, one he had found in Douglas's bedroom. Its serial number matched the one Douglas had reported missing. He laid it carefully on the table beside his chair.

"What you are doing, Officer Douglas, is killing people in cold blood."

"Criminals, gangsters, people who laugh at the law and who deserve to die, the same kind of people who you gun down in cold blood."

"Listen to me, Douglas, I have not killed anyone who did not have a gun in his hand, wasn't reaching for a gun, or was not in some way about to try and kill me. Anyone I've killed has had an even or better chance at me. That's what the law you mentioned demands. You shot unarmed men, some in the back, without giving them that chance."

"Scum like them don't deserve a chance, why should we give them one?"

"Because we're the good guys."

"There's not much difference between you and me, Devil."

"It's a fine line, yes, but the line is there, Douglas, and you crossed it. It's time to go."

"Go where, Devil?"

Devlin realized that Douglas did not, and would never, understand the difference between the two of them. Later, in his darker moments, when he allowed himself to really think about what he did as the Devil, Devlin worried that that line he mentioned was beginning to fade for him.

The Devil stood up and positioned himself across the room from Douglas. He'd give the man his chance, the same one he'd give anyone else.

"Brian Douglas, you are under arrest for the murder of David Fulton and four others."

"I'm a cop, Devlin, I can't go to prison."

"I'm a cop, too, Brian. I can't let you walk."

"That's it then?"

"That's it."

Both men drew at the same time, but Devlin was rested while Douglas had just worked sixteen hours in the last twenty-four. Before Douglas could clear his holster, the Devil's shot took him down.

It was over. Douglas's death would be listed as line of duty, if only to spare his family. The deaths for which he was responsible would remain "unsolved," but the Commissioner would later hint to the papers that they were mob related, just to sow doubt and confusion among the gangs. Frank Devlin was officially cleared of any suspicion, and stalked the streets unrivalled as the only Devil

Harbor City would ever know.

Chapter Four
The Devil's Judgement

For Dr. Sidney Marcus, Monday started as a good day, with the promise of being the start of an even better week. For the first time since he opened his practice six months ago, he had a full schedule of patients. His secretary Cheryl had returned from vacation, which meant that he was free of the temporary worker the agency had sent in her place. The temp had been a nice girl, willing to work and eager to please in what seemed to be her first job, but somehow she just could not catch on to the routine of a doctor's office. The first week went all right, but in the second week she had been distracted, unable to concentrate on her work. She forgot to record appointments and copy messages, and twice she had left patients leave without paying. She had been worried about something, but when Marcus asked, she had brushed it off as trouble with her boyfriend and "one of those woman things." Knowing little about women except how to cure their physical ills, the doctor let the matter drop.

He could have, he supposed, called the agency and had the girl replaced. But he was not long out of medical school himself, and he remembered his residency, when he was an intern who made as many mistakes as diagnoses. Rather than put a mark against her record, he simply waited out the week.

Marcus had finished checking his instruments and making sure everything was ready for his patients. He could hear Cheryl in the outer office making her preparations. When she had come in that morning, he told her his tale of woe about her replacement. She promised to have things set straight by the afternoon break, and jokingly suggested that if she was that important to the practice he should make her a partner.

A bell rang. That would be the first patient of the day coming through the outer door. Marcus checked his watch. Seven thirty, his patient was a half an hour early. Well, it was always good to start a busy day a little ahead of schedule.

"Can I help you, sir?" Cheryl's pleasant voice came through his door, not at all like the nasal twang of that temporary. How, Marcus wondered, could it be? Cheryl and her replacement bore a physical similarity, but looks aside, they were nothing alike.

Cheryl's scream interrupted his reverie. As he rushed to her aid there was a loud bang in the outer office. He opened the connecting door and saw a young man standing at Cheryl's desk. He was neatly dressed in a grey suit, and could have been any of the men who worked in the building where Marcus had his practice. Then Marcus saw the gun.

Marcus glanced over toward where Cheryl should have been sitting. Her chair was empty, but the spatters of red on the wall behind her desk left him no doubt as to her fate. He looked down, and saw her feet sticking out from the far end of the desk.

"Sorry, Doc," the young man spoke, taking Marcus's attention away from his fallen secretary. "Nothing personal, but you shouldn't have come out of your office." As the young man turned the gun toward Marcus, the doctor's last thought was that maybe it wasn't going to be such a good day after all.

After blowing the doctor back into the examination room, Brody got to wondering if maybe he should have used a silencer, or at least a smaller gun. The noise from the big .45 had filled the office and Brody was sure that the whole building had heard it.

Brody didn't know that the Hamilton Medical Center had been built with quiet in mind. The thickness of the walls made each office suite just about soundproof. The group of physicians who had had it built at the end of the last century had made sure that even the loudest screams coming from one doctor's office would not disturb patients in another. All Brody knew was that he had just made a lot of noise and should leave as quickly as possible.

A shame about the doc, Brody thought. He had been told to make sure that there were no witnesses to his hit on the secretary. When the doctor came out from the back, that made him a witness and Brody always followed orders.

Brody slowly opened the outer door of the office and peeked down the hallway. He was expecting a rush of people coming to see what all the noise was all about. He was mildly puzzled but very grateful when the hallway proved to be empty.

He kept his gun down by his side as he walked toward the stairs. He did not encounter anyone until he reached the fourth floor lobby. Then, just as he had opened the door to the stairwell, a bell rang and two witnesses stepped off the elevator.

Brody had turned at the sound of the bell and watched as the elevator doors opened. A young girl and an older man stepped off. Caught up in their conversation, neither one took note of the young man in the grey suit. Brody, of course, could not be sure that he had gone unnoticed and, repeating "No witnesses" as a kind of mantra, opened fire.

The first two shots blew the young girl back into the elevator. As the doors closed behind her, the older man rushed the killer.

The older man had been in the war, had faced gunfire before. He knew that to run was to catch a bullet in the back. His only hope was to surprise the gunman and overpower him before he could get off another shot. It was a false hope, however. Brody's next two shots took him in the head and chest.

Brody opened the stairwell door and began his escape down the four flights of steps. He stopped only twice, once to take care of a witness who had foolishly decided, for health reasons, to take the stairs rather than the elevator, and once to load a fresh clip of ammo in his weapon.

By this time, the sound of gunfire had been heard throughout the building. People in the first floor lobby waiting for the elevator were becoming edgy, some were beginning to panic. The security guard was busy trying to both calm the crowd and call the police. Just then, the elevator door opened.

The guard pushed his way through the waiting people and drew his gun, prepared to meet whoever came off. The body of a blood stained young girl dropped at his feet.

He heard a thump as an elderly woman fell to the floor behind him. He then turned and ordered everyone else out of the building. Making sure that they were safely out, he went back for the fallen women.

The younger of the two, the one who had fallen out of the elevator, was clearly dead. He ignored her, holstered his weapon and picked up the elderly woman. As he stood, Brody came out of the stairwell door and into the lobby.

Without hesitation the guard dropped the woman and went for his gun. Brody's gun, however, was already drawn. "No witnesses" was the last thing the guard heard before Brody blew his life away.

Brody turned his gun on the fallen and now bruised woman lying on the floor. He was about to fire when he saw that she was unconscious and thus could not have witnessed anything. He withheld his fire and turned to the exit.

Through the glass of the front doors Brody could see a crowd of people, all watching the drama inside. Why they had not fled when Brody killed the guard he did not know, but he did know that there were now too many witnesses. He emptied his clip into the front doors. Bullets flew and glass shattered. People fell, killed and injured by flying lead and broken glass. Others fled, leaving the scene to the approaching police cars.

Deafened by repeated gunfire, Brody could not hear the sirens. Just the same, he knew that the police had to be on their way. He decided against leaving the front way and instead turned back to the stairwell, hoping that there was an exit through the basement.

Brody got lucky. The back door of the basement was open and lead to an alley in the rear of the building. No janitor was in sight, and so Brody left the building without having to worry about any more witnesses. By the time the police found their way to the rear,

Brody was gone.

There were so many police cars on the scene that Devlin had to park his a block away. As he walked toward the Hamilton Building, he could see that the newshounds had already gathered. The reporters would be desperate to talk to anyone who could tell them what had happened, while the photographers would be scheming to get inside, so that pictures of the carnage could sell more papers. Money would change hands before this day was out, and more than one cop would get his name in the paper.

Devlin's chief concern about the newspapermen present was that none of them recognized him. To them, Frank Devlin was "The Devil," Harbor City's official avenger, specially appointed by the Police Commissioner himself to hunt down and punish those criminals whom the law could not touch. Today, however, he was just another cop, specially appointed by the Police Commissioner himself to find out what had happened at the medical building and to report on the progress of the investigation. If, later, the killer was identified and somehow escaped justice, then the Devil would join the hunt, but not before. Today, Devlin had other concerns to worry about.

When Devlin first became a patrolman, the Harbor City Police were at war with the local gangs. The mobs operated openly, protected by corrupt judges and dependent politicians. The public ignored the situation, seeing it a game of cops and robbers played out in the papers instead of on a movie screen. After Devlin became "The Devil," things improved somewhat. The gang leaders were still in power, less the two Devlin had had to kill, but they were not as blatant in their operations. No longer did the average citizen have to worry about being caught in crossfire between two rival mobs. "There'll be the Devil to pay" was taken literally in Harbor City when an innocent bystander was killed in a shootout.

But the war continued. Criminals whom the police arrested

could count on finding either an assistant D.A. or a judge who had some connection to one of the mobs. The Chief Magistrate and the District Attorney did what they could to weed out the corruption, but it's hard to get rid of a politically appointed judge, and the replacements for the fired prosecutors were all just as young, just as underpaid, and just as susceptible to the temptation of big money as their predecessors.

"I can't just kill them all." Devlin thought back to that morning's interrupted conversation with the Commissioner.

"No one's asking you to, Frank."

"But how else are we going to stop it? We arrest the crooks. Then either an A.D.A. on the take drops or lowers the charges, or else a bent judge dismisses the case or gives probation for what should be a twenty-year term. No matter how many of them go down, more take their place. Sometimes it feels like I'm not making a difference."

The Commissioner looked at the young man sitting across from him. He knew the toll that being the Devil was taking on him. Taking lives is not as easy as cheap paperbacks sold in the corner store made it seem. And Devlin had killed more men than most.

"Son, I've told you before that you're just one part of this war. I have people working on the inside at the D.A.'s office and the courthouse. They are gathering the evidence we need to bring charges of bribery, malfeasance, obstruction of justice, and accessory before and after the fact of every sort of crime. Sooner or later we'll sweep them all them up. Don't forget, Al Capone went down on tax charges."

Devlin smiled. "So now I'm Elliot Ness?"

"Exactly. You keep them busy and distracted. I'll take out their support system. Together we'll bring them down.

"Now then, Frank, what are you working on?"

Devlin had started to fill the Chief in on his continuing search for the missing gang boss Anthony Peterson when the telephone rang with news of the massacre. Devlin left soon after.

As Devlin approached the front of the building, the first things he saw were several cloth-covered mounds. *The first of many victims,* he thought as he felt the Devil rise up inside him.

"There's at least one more to go," he said aloud when he thought of catching up with the killer. By this time, he was closer and he could see the rope marking the boundaries of the scene. There were rookie cops just outside this line, keeping the press and other curious parties from crossing over. He could see the shattered glass of the front door and hear the noises of investigation coming from the building.

Devlin walked up to the nearest uniform and before he could be challenged, flashed his gold badge.

"Commissioner's office, where's the officer in charge?"

"Around the side, Sergeant." The rookie pointed to the far end of the building. "There's a second entrance there." The young cop looked down at the bodies in front of the doors. "This one's sort of blocked."

Devlin thanked the young officer, stepped under the rope, and quickly made his way to the side entrance. Devlin showed his ID to the officer on guard, and was directed down the hall and to a vacant office, where the investigating detectives had set up a makeshift headquarters. The three men in that office turned as Devlin came through the door.

"If it isn't the Devil himself," said the oldest man, the one clearly in charge. "What's the matter, Devlin? The Chief don't think we've got enough bodies lying around, he sent you to make more."

The other two men held their breath. Within the department, Devlin's reputation as a man killer had grown into a dark legend. Most cops either feared or avoided him, or else treated him with the kind of respect usually reserved for the top command. So far, none had dared joked with him about his recent activities.

"No, Campbell, the Boss figures you got enough to do with my making more work for you." Devlin walked over to a window and looked out at the crowd. "Unless you want me to take out a reporter or two. How about Smith over there?"

"Thanks, but the Lab boys have already finished up out there. They don't need you adding to their work. Besides, Smith's promised to make me as big a hero as you when I solve this case."

Devlin smiled, glad to be one of the boys again, however briefly. "Some other time then."

With the ice broken, Devlin got down to business. "What have you got?"

"Well, I can tell you, or I can give you the tour."

"The tour, I think, Sergeant Campbell."

Campbell talked as he led Devlin down the hall to the lobby. "We got twelve dead, ten from gunshots. You already saw the five outside. One of them got his throat cut by flying glass when our shooter unloaded through the front door. Here in the lobby you got three down. The old lady there ain't got a mark on her. The doc figures a heart attack, probably when the girl there fell out of the elevator."

Taking the stairs, Campbell took Devlin up to the fourth floor, along the way pointing out the body on the third floor landing and the one lying just outside the elevator door after they got to the fourth. "That's number ten." Campbell said. "The last two are down here in corner office."

Once in Marcus's office, Campbell gave Devlin the okay to look around. "Just be careful about touching things," the homicide cop added. "The Lab guys haven't had a chance to check for prints."

Hands in pockets, Devlin nodded. He looked passed the body of the doctor into the examination room. As Campbell talked, Devlin walked over and studied the top of the secretary's desk.

"We figure this is where it all started. The killer was here for an appointment, something set him off and he killed these two. Then he left, taking out anybody who might be able to ID him. Or maybe he was just a nut case who didn't like doctors, and this was the only open office."

Campbell was talking more to himself than to Devlin, trying to make some sense out of a dozen deaths. Knowing this, Devlin let him spin his theories. When the investigator paused for a breath, Devlin cut in.

"First three appointments are all for women, the first one of those at eight." He looked down at a spent casing on the desk. "Most women don't carry .45s, much less spare clips like you found on the stairs."

Devlin looked up at Campbell, saw no reaction in the detective's face and went on. "There are doctors in this building who see patients as early as six, and we're on the fourth floor. Our boy came up here for a reason, and that was to kill one or both of the people in this room.

"How am I doing so far?"

Campbell smiled. "Pretty good for a guy who never worked homicide. You figured it the same as I did. This was a hit. The others just got in the way."

"Most mob guys aren't this sloppy. They'd just ..."

"Devlin, you okay?"

Devlin had been looking at the dead body of the secretary as he talked. He had idly noted that, according to her desk calendar, she had just that day returned from vacation. He was thinking that she should have taken another week off when he started thinking like the Devil.

How would I do it, he thought. How would I take out two men without being seen coming in or going out? The going out was easy. Devlin had ten examples of that between himself and the street, but the coming in?

"Devlin?"

"Oh, Campbell, yeah, I'm okay, excuse me." Devlin brushed passed the other cop and went into the hallway.

"It's down the hall and to the right. Mention my name and you'll get a good seat."

"Thanks, Campbell, but I went before I came here." Devlin had stopped just outside the office and was looking down the hallway. Seeing what he was looking for, he walked over to an office a few doors down.

"This place vacant?"

"There's nobody in there. We did do a search."

"I'm sure, but is it being used?"

"Don't look like it, no name on the door."

Devlin went in. He noted a chair sitting at an odd angle to the door, sat in it, then got up and closed the door until it was open just a crack. He sat back down and looked through the narrow opening. He could still see the entire hallway, and if anyone was coming his way.

Devlin got up, saw two more chairs that had been arranged to face each other. They were separated just enough for someone to get a good night's sleep. Finally, in a trashcan in the back room, he found a crumpled paper bag and wax paper, an empty juice bottle, the remains of a sandwich and a half-eaten apple.

Campbell had been watching him all along. To the homicide cop Devlin said, "Your man spent the night here. He snuck in here last evening, as the place was closing down. He brought a lunch and stayed the night. This morning he woke up, waited until the time was right, walked down the hall and did it."

Campbell was clearly impressed. "Forget about pretty good. You ever want to be murder police, I want to be your partner."

"Thanks. You get the Lab in here to dust for prints you'll probably get your man."

"Yeah, the bottle, the wax paper, the chair arms. If there's a bathroom in here he probably used that once or twice. Get some good prints in there.

"Tell me something, Devlin."

"What's that?"

"You didn't just guess at this, you knew where to go and what you'd find. How did you now he hid in here?"

"It's how I would have done it."

Leaving Campbell in the spare office, Devlin found one that wasn't a part of the crime scene and called the Commissioner. When he got back, the homicide man was giving instructions to the uniformed officer who was guarding the fourth floor.

"When they get up here, tell the lab boys that I want both these offices done." Campbell pointed first to the doctor's office then to the one where the killer had spent the night. "Tell them to work overtime, or call in extra people if they have to, but I want the prints from these two places in the Identification Section tonight." Campbell turned to Devlin.

"What did the Chief say?"

"He said to keep up the good work. He wants me back at HQ so I can brief him so he can brief the press. You're to tell the vultures outside that he'll make a statement within the hour. That'll get most out of them out of your hair. Oh, and he wants a list of any bodies you've ID'd."

"He's not going to release that, is he?"

Devlin shook his head. "He just wants to start to notify the families, one thing less that you'll have to worry about."

"Thank God for that, I hate that job."

Campbell walked Devlin back down stairs, then gave the list of known dead. Devlin folded it, stuck it in his coat pocket. He waited until Campbell made his announcement to the reporters outside and watched them scatter towards their cars, all wanting to be up front for the Commissioner's briefing. "Like roaches when the light goes on," Devlin whispered to the uniform guarding the police line as he ducked under it on his way to his car. Thankful that this was one case he didn't have to worry about, he drove back to Headquarters.

Back in the Commissioner's office, Devlin gave him the list. The Chief dismissed him and he turned to go. He had the door partway open when he was called back.

"Frank, did you bother to read this?"

"No, sir. I took it from Campbell and brought it straight to you."

The Commissioner held it out and Devlin took it. "Read the fourth name down."

"Maria Boroni." Devlin handed the list back. "The old woman who died from heart failure. Should I know the name?" he asked.

"No reason you should, before your time. Her husband used to be in the rackets, before he was killed. Her maiden name was Martinelli."

It was odd to find Martinelli's restaurant closed on a Saturday night. The last time that that had happened was when Antonio Martinelli was killed. His nephew Louis took over the family business, both sides of it. He closed the restaurant the day before his uncle's funeral. He reopened it a week afterwards. In those seven days, everyone who could have had a hand in Antonio Martinelli's death died. Devlin studied the black wreath on the front door and hoped that tonight he could forestall a similar bloodbath.

Devlin found a spot on the door not covered by the wreath and knocked on the door. His knock was answered by Nicholas, the maître d', who had just moved aside to admit the sergeant when a young woman entered the lobby from the dining area.

"Who is that, Nicholas?" she asked.

"Sergeant Devlin, Miss Angela, from the police."

"I know who Sergeant Devlin is, Nicholas." She turned and stepped in front of the detective, blocking his way. "You're the one they call 'the Devil,' aren't you? Well, there's no one for you to kill in here. Just go and leave my family in peace. The police have no business here, especially not tonight. You should be out looking for the monster that killed my aunt."

Her family. Then this must Angela Martinelli, Louis's daughter. Devlin had heard that she was back from school in Europe. She was not Devlin had expected. Instead of the dark Italian features of her father, Angela was a testament to her mother's Dublin background. Her green eyes and red hair were nicely set off by the black dress she wore, and the spray of freckles across her nose were not what Devlin thought off when he pictured a gangster's daughter.

He would have told her of his reason for coming to the restaurant, but he could not find the room to interrupt. Instead, he let her tirade continue, sure that she would talk herself out. Instead he waited, and listened to the curious mixture of Sicilian and Celtic that accented her speech.

"Well?" Angela had stopped, and Devlin had not been aware of it. Or rather, he had been too aware of her and not what she was saying. "Will you be leaving, Mr. Devlin?"

"No, the sergeant will not be leaving, Angela." Martinelli's voice came from the dining area. "Nicholas, will you please bring Sergeant Devlin into the private dining area. I will join you shortly."

Nicholas led Devlin to the same table where he had once asked Martinelli's help in stopping a gang war. Martinelli joined him soon after. He brought a bottle of wine to the table. He opened it and poured two glasses, giving one to Devlin. The two men drank in silence, Devlin content to wait on his host.

Martinelli emptied and refilled his glass. Devlin's was still half full but he let Martinelli top it off. After taking another drink, the gang leader spoke.

"I know why you are here, Sergeant. You have come to warn me against seeking vengeance for the death of my aunt. You will tell me that the police are best able to bring this madman to justice, and that any action I may take could only jeopardize the investigation. You will wish me to be patient, and allow the police to their job."

Devlin nodded his head in agreement. "First of all, Mr. Martinelli, allow me to express my sympathies for your loss of a family member. It is always painful to lose a close relative, and I can understand why you would want to punish the killer yourself. If Mrs. Boroni were my aunt, I would feel the same."

Devlin took a sip of wine, the continued. "That said, I did come here tonight to ask you to be patient, to give us time to find this man. We will soon know who he is. Once we do, we will find him and learn why he did what he did. The involvement of your people could only cause trouble."

"I fail to see how, Sergeant, if we are both looking for the same man it will double the chances of finding him."

"Your involvement, Mr. Martinelli, could cause you trouble with me, and neither of us want that."

Martinelli considered Devlin's threat. He had no problems with defying the police, but he did not want to fight the Devil.

"My problem, Sergeant," he finally said, "is this. A member of my family has been killed. That is an affront to the family honor, and a challenge to me personally. If I do not act, if I rely on the police, I will be seen as weak, and weakness if fatal in this city."

"So is going against the Devil."

Martinelli was silent for a time. Finally, he came to a decision. "Some time ago, sergeant, you sat at this table and asked me a favor. I did you that favor, and together we stopped a gang war. Tonight, you ask another favor. Now, I ask you for a favor in return."

Despite his sorrow over the death of his aunt, Devlin could hear the steel that was always in Martinelli's voice. Devlin knew what he was going to ask. It was the only option for either of them.

"Tonight, Sergeant Devlin, I am asking you for the same justice that you would give to my kind. I want the Devil to find this man, this man who killed my aunt and those others. The Devil, not Campbell or anyone else. Find him, and make him pay for this sin."

"If the killer is identified, I will look for him. If I find him, I will do what I must."

"If it the Devil who finds him, then I will be satisfied. If not, if he lives to be arrested, then I would appreciate some advance word."

As he knew they would be, these were Devlin's choices. Kill the suspect himself, or allow Martinelli to do it later. Even as he was walking to the restaurant, Devlin worried about the deal he would have to make. Would he agree to kill a man for Louis Martinelli? Or would he be doing his job, letting Martinelli think what he liked. If he agreed to tell Martinelli when a suspect was in custody, the man would not live more than a few days after his arrest. Yet, if a suspect's arrest was kept from Martinelli, his sense of family honor would turn the city into a slaughterhouse as he looked for a man who had already been found. And what if the wrong man is arrested? Devlin did not want to think about that.

Devlin told himself that he would be doing nothing illegal, nothing that would not be done for the families of the other eleven victims. The thought did not comfort him. He finally decided that no matter the circumstances, this killer of twelve people deserved to die. Whether the State, the Devil, or Martinelli did it, the Devil really didn't care.

"And so what if Martinelli does the State's job?" asked that part of him that was the Devil. "Whoever it is, he deserves to die. My job is to take out this city's garbage however I can. Martinelli is just a weapon I can use."

To Martinelli, Devlin said quietly, "Naturally, the families of the deceased will be notified as soon as possible."

"Thank you, Sergeant, I believe that I can be patient for a few days. I wish you luck."

On his way out, Devlin stopped to talk to Angela Martinelli.

"Ms. Martinelli, I am very sorry for intruding on your family at a time like this. There were however, some matters regarding your aunt's death that your father and I had to discuss."

"I understand, Sergeant, and please forgive me for the way I spoke to you earlier. You will find this killer for us, won't you?" Her voice now was softer, not friendly, but at least not hostile. Nicholas must have told her of his relationship with her father. Or else, she'd been listening.

"I'll do all that I can, Miss Martinelli," he promised as he slipped out the door.

IV

Two days later Devlin found himself knocking on the door to the chambers of the Honorable Steven Calvert, Judge of the

Circuit Court of Harbor City.

"Can I help you?"

"I'm Detective Sergeant Francis Devlin, here to see the judge."

The law clerk that answered the door seemed to take offense that anyone would dare to address his boss as simply "the judge."

"His Honor," Devlin could hear the capitals in the clerk's voice, "is a very busy man. Do you have an appointment?"

"No, but I have a badge and a gun, and I'm here on police business. Will you tell *His Honor* that I would like a few moments of his time?"

"I am afraid that Judge Calvert is working on some briefs at the moment and cannot be disturbed, no matter what the reason. If you would like to make an appointment, he might be able to fit you in sometime tomorrow."

The clerk had just finished speaking when the sound of giggling came from the inner chamber. This was followed by several high-pitched squeals of delight. The clerk tried to ignore the sounds but could not ignore the look on Devlin's face.

"Go tell *His Honor* that he has five minutes to adjust his briefs and then I'm coming in."

The clerk picked up the telephone, buzzed the inner chamber and withstood a minute of verbal abuse. When he managed to interrupt, he told the judge, "There's a police detective to see you, sir. He says it's very urgent."

"Remind him about his briefs," prompted Devlin.

"No sir, I don't think it can wait . . . I'll ask." To Devlin he said, "What was your name again, Sergeant?"

"Just tell him the Devil's come to call."

Once in the judge's chambers Devlin gave no sign of what he had heard some minutes before. Nor did he mention the attractive young woman who had left the room just prior to his entry. The judge on his part gave the appearance that Devlin had interrupted important business, which, Devlin supposed, he had.

"So you're the Devil?"

"To some, Your Honor, to some."

"And what brings the Devil to my door?"

"Your Honor, you no doubt have heard about the murders at the Hamilton Medical Center two days ago."

"Yes, I have, a terrible thing. You're here for a warrant? You've solved the case then?"

"We do have some answers, yes, but I'm not here for a warrant."

"What then?" The judge motioned Devlin to sit down.

"Your Honor, do you remember William Brody?"

Judge Calvert thought for a moment. "The name is familiar, but I cannot place it. Should I remember it?"

"Last week he appeared before you in an assault case. He was accused of beating a woman who had refused to go out with him. He pled guilty and received a three year suspended sentence."

"Yes, I remember, why?"

"Well, Your Honor, our evidence suggests that this William Brody was the man who committed the murders."

The judge was visibly shaken. His face went pale, and his hands started to shake. "You're sure of this?" His voice was not as strong as it had been moments ago.

"We found his prints are all over the crime scene." In the room where he hid out, Devlin could have added, but he did not want to give the judge too many details.

Devlin gave the judge a few minutes to compose himself before speaking again. "Your Honor, I have to ask, did you receive any inducement to give Brody that suspended sentence?" Calvert's face went from white to red as Devlin spoke. "Any threat or bribe, anything like …"

"How dare you suggest such a thing?" Judge Calvert rose from his chair as if to come across the desk at Devlin. "You have no right to suspect me."

Devlin had risen to meet the judge's probable attack when the judge just as suddenly sat down again. Devlin resumed his seat and waited. Finally, Calvert spoke.

"I apologize, Detective. This, of course, is Harbor City, and, considering the past behavior of my fellow jurists, you have every right to ask that question.

"No, I received no bribe, threat or any promise of either. I judged that case solely on its merits. The assault, such as it was, was a mere placing of hands. Brody had met the woman in a nightclub and asked her out. She said no and tried to leave. Brody grabbed her by the arm and she screamed. Charges were pressed, etc. In court, Brody expressed remorse. Under the circumstances the sentence was proper."

"Did you know that Brody had a prior criminal record?"

"Who doesn't in this town? Yes, I knew. He had convictions for robbery, burglary, and a previous assault. But he'd been clean for over a year. I had hoped that he had truly reformed, and that this matter was a simple lapse. I see that I was tragically wrong."

Devlin rose to leave. "And you'll take your lumps in the press for it."

"That I will, Detective, that I will. It's a good thing I don't stand for reelection for another eight years."

Calvert held out his hand to Devlin. "Thank you for coming. When you catch him, take him down hard."

Taking the hand, Devlin said, "I intend to. Thank you for your understanding."

Devlin turned to go when the judge stopped him. "One more thing, Detective Devlin. They call you the Devil."

"Yes, Sir, they do."

"You earned that name fighting the gangs that plague our city, correct?"

"Yes, sir."

"Why then are you investigating a homicide, that's a bit out of your line, isn't it."

Devlin told the judge about Maria Boroni.

Judge Calvert realized what that meant. "He'll tear this city apart looking for her killer."

"That he will, Your Honor, that he will. One of Martinelli's few redeeming virtues is a fierce loyalty to friends and family, especially family. It's my job to find Brody and take him down hard and fast, to keep peace in the city."

"Good luck to you, Detective."

"Thank you, I'll need it."

V

Devlin wanted to find Brody fast not only to prevent a possible blood bath but to get to him before Martinelli had him killed. Only Brody knew who had hired him, and Devlin wanted that knowledge. From the position of the bodies, the secretary at her desk and the doctor coming through the door, it appeared as if the hit had been on the woman. Campbell was right now checking leads on who might have wanted her dead. Find Brody, apply some pressure, and get the name. If it was the right name, it might help bring down one of the major mob bosses. Still, there was something about the setup that was bothering Devlin. There was an answer he did not have, a question he did not know to ask.

"I'll leave the thinking to Campbell and his boys," he thought. "I'll just find Brody and let the Devil do his work."

The information about Brody's presence on the crime scene was kept from the press. So was Devlin's part in the case. With no hint that anyone was looking for him, Brody made himself ridiculously easy to find.

Brody had quit his job and moved. While the homicide squad tried to trace him through friends and family, Devlin took a different approach. Brody was in the third bar he checked.

The bar was crowded. Wednesday was payday for a lot of Harbor City laborers, and it seemed as if most of them had stopped in Moby's to drink up all or part of their checks. Brody was sitting at a table against the far wall, under a picture of a great white whale. The whale was standing on his fins, holding a harpoon in his right flipper, picking his teeth with it. In his left flipper, he held a one-legged sea captain. A caption at the bottom read, "Don't Mess with Moby."

Devlin looked around the room. He did not see anyone else

he recognized as part of Harbor City's crime scene. The bartender, a large fat man after whom the place was obviously named, was busy serving customers and did not appear to be on the lookout for anyone in particular.

Brody was feeling good. He had a new place to live, much nicer than his old one. He had a drink in front of him and money in his pocket, and more of both back home. He felt sure that, with the help of his newly earned fortune, he could attract the attention of a pretty lady or two before the night was out. Best of all, he had his freedom. A week ago, he had none of these, and now he was sitting pretty. William Brody was indeed feeling very good.

It was while Brody was enjoying his good feeling that a man came across the room and stood in front of his table. This man blocked Brody's view of the rest of the bar. Brody looked up and almost recognized him. Brody had seen his face before, and he seemed to be someone Brody should have known.

"Hello, Willie. Ready to pay for your sins?" Devlin slid the table tight against Brody's chest

Recognition set in. "Oh my God, it's you, the Devil. But how? There weren't any witnesses." Trapped by the table, Brody could barely move. He struggled to get at the gun under his arm. Devlin drew his own weapon and held it close to his chest, down on the table, out of view of the rest of the bar.

"Don't do it, Willie. Believe it or not, I'd really rather not have to kill you. Now, let's talk."

Brody had gotten his hand on his weapon, but the pressure of the table on his gun arm was such that he could not draw it. He saw the Devil's gun pointed straight at his heart. He was halfway between trying again to draw and giving up when he somehow pulled the trigger.

The blast from the .45 missed all of Brody and blew a big hole in the wall behind him. The unexpected noise surprised Devlin enough that he relaxed his hold on the table. With the pressure off, Brody pushed the table away and brought his gun up.

Devlin had no choice. As much as he needed the name of

Brody's boss, he did not want it bad enough to get shot for it. He fired twice, and Brody went down.

The Devil stepped back and let Brody fall. As he did, he looked around the room. Most of the patrons had fled, those that hadn't had taken whatever cover they could find. The bartender, however, pulled a shotgun out from behind the bar and was bringing it to bear on Devlin.

The Devil fired a shot in his direction, aiming to miss. "Don't do it, Moby, or there'll be blubber all over the bar." Moby's shotgun quickly hit the floor.

"Good, now call the police." Devlin showed his badge and Moby turned to the telephone.

Devlin now bent over the fallen Brody. The killer was still breathing, but both knew these were his last breaths.

"Who was it, Brody? Who hired you to kill the girl?"

"Tell him, no witnesses. I made sure, no witnesses."

"I'll tell him, Brody, who is it?" No reply. Brody, the last witness, was dead.

A few hours later, Devlin sat with Campbell as the two men watched the photographer from the Crime Lab take the last of his pictures.

"You know, Frank, you don't always have to kill them. A lot of police simply arrest the bad guy and let the courts deal with them."

"I could have let him kill me, but then you guys would have just had to find him all over again."

"You could have called for back up. You could have called me and we would have taken him when he stepped outside. Hero or no hero, you're going to wish he had killed you when the Chief gets through with you. This guy could have broken things wide open. He was an important witness and you killed him."

Devlin looked over at Moby pulling himself a beer and wished he were off duty. "Tell me about it. Or rather don't. The Chief's going to give me plenty tomorrow. Wait . . ."

"For what?"

"Witness. You said witness, Brody kept saying witnesses. That's the key to this. Cheryl Bloom may have been killed because she witnessed something."

"Probably, why else are innocent people killed in this city. But Frank, what could she have witnessed? She was out of town the two weeks before she was killed."

Both men slowly looked at each other as they realized what Campbell had said.

Diane Hollander was not surprised to see the two detectives at her door, she only wondered what had taken them so long.

Judge Steven Calvert walked into his courtroom. His mind on other matters, he only vaguely heard the bailiff's shout of "All rise." He sat down and told the crowd that it could do likewise.

"Call the first case, if you please, Bailiff."

From his post next to the bench, the bailiff began his shout of "The People call …" when he was interrupted by a voice from the back of the room.

"The Devil calls the case against Judge Steven Calvert."

The courtroom fell silent. Attorneys stopped their bargaining. Reporters who had been told that something interesting would happen began writing furiously. Frank Devlin came forward and walked to the front of the courtroom. Standing in front of the bench, he waited quietly for the judge's outburst.

"What is the meaning of this, Sergeant? Is this some kind of a joke?"

"It is no joke, Your Honor. You stand accused of the deaths of a dozen people. How do you plead, guilty or not?"

"Sergeant Devlin, explain yourself this minute, or I'll find you in contempt of this court."

"I already hold this court in contempt. Now, are you ready to pay for your sins?"

"Guards, seize this man."

None of the guards moved. The judge then realized that these were not the regular courtroom guards. They were, instead, men that Devlin had put into place before the morning session had started.

Devlin turned his back to the bench and addressed the crowd. "If it please the Court. Last week there was a massacre at the Hamilton Medical Center. A man named William Brody killed a secretary because somebody paid him to do so. He killed ten other people because they got in his way. Another woman died of a heart attack.

"Why did this happen? It happened because a week before, there was an accident outside the medical center. A small boy was struck and seriously injured by a speeding car. The driver did not stop. No witnesses came forth."

Devlin turned and addressed Calvert. "How am I doing so far, Judge?"

Judge Calvert looked at Devlin coldly. "I have no idea what you're talking about."

Devlin smiled. "Just wait, it gets better."

He again addressed the crowd. "No witnesses came forth," he repeated. "But there was a witness, wasn't there, Judge?" Devlin turned back to the bench, the people behind him now forgotten. "One who saw you clearly. One who recognized you from all those times you got your picture in the paper. One who called you up and told you what she saw.

"What did she want? Did she threaten you with blackmail? No, I think that she just wanted to give you the chance to come forward on your own. To do the right thing.

"And what did you do? You found out where she worked, and sent William Brody to take care of the only witness against you. In exchange, you let Brody walk on an assault charge and paid him for his trouble."

Devlin stopped. He knew Calvert had to answer the charge and he was waiting for the judge's denials.

"An interesting theory, Sergeant. One with no basis in fact, but an interesting theory."

"But, Your Honor, there is some basis in fact."

"What proof do you have, Devlin? The secretary is dead. Brody is dead, killed by your own hand. You have no proof."

"If it please the Court, the Devil calls Diane Hollander."

Sergeant Campbell led Miss Hollander into the courtroom. As he brought her to the witness stand, Devlin explained, "You see, Judge, Brody killed the wrong secretary.

"This woman before you was the one who saw you run down the child. She called you, and told you that she was working in Dr. Marcus's office. What she did not tell you was that she was only there for the rest of that week. When you told Brody to kill Marcus's secretary, he did. It just wasn't Miss Hollander."

By now, Campbell had Diane Hollander on the witness chair. With a nod from Devlin, he administered the oath. "Do you swear to tell the truth, the whole truth, and nothing but the truth, so help you God?"

"I do!"

"Your witness, Devil."

"Miss Hollander, is the man in the black robe the one you saw run down a child in front of the Hamilton Medical Center nine days ago?"

"He is."

"Your witness, Your Honor."

"I refuse to go along with this farce any longer." Judge Calvert got up and left the bench. Devlin's guards, however, prevented him from leaving the courtroom. They instead brought him over to Devlin.

"I take it the defense rests?" Devlin looked from Calvert up to the empty bench.

I've gone this far, he thought. I might as well do it right. He walked passed Calvert and took the vacant seat. Picking up the gavel, he banged it twice.

"This court finds Judge Steven Calvert responsible for the deaths of the dozen people at the Hamilton Medical Center. He is responsible for the ten people dead of gunshots, responsible for the man whose throat was cut, responsible for causing the fatal heart attack of Maria Boroni, beloved aunt and godmother of Louis Martinelli, one of Harbor City's more prominent citizens."

Devlin looked up and addressed the reporters who were now crowding the front row. "Did you get that last part, boys?"

To Calvert, he said, "There is, however, no direct evidence linking you to this crime. All witnesses to it are dead. It is the decision of this court that you be set free to live as long as you can. May you enjoy your final hours."

Devlin banged the gavel again. "This court is adjourned."

Devlin had known that he could not prove Calvert's guilt in a courtroom. He also knew that Martinelli would not need the proof that the law required. Now that the man responsible for his aunt's death was identified, he would act. Calvert may be alive for now, but The Devil's judgement meant death, and that sentence was always carried out.

Chapter Five
Deal with the Devil

Things had not been going very well for the Honorable Judge Steven Calvert. Last month, a ruling on which he had done considerable research and had spent an enormous amount of time was overturned by the State Supreme Court as "having no constitutional basis." Shortly after that, after spending an enjoyable night at the apartment of his mistress, he learned that it was over. She was moving out of state, she told him. She was starting a new life, one that did not include married men. On his drive to the courtroom, Calvert was worried that she would call his wife. Tired from lack of sleep, distracted by the break-up, afraid for his marriage, the judge failed to see a young boy crossing the street on his way to school.

His car hit the boy and sent him flying to the sidewalk. The judge almost stopped, but then thought about the cost to himself. He'd be identified, his name would be in the papers. He'd have to explain why he was driving to court from downtown instead of his suburban home. His wife would want to know why he was driving at all, as he supposed to have spent the night in his chambers after an important late night judicial conference.

He slowed down instead. Looking around, he could see that the street was empty. There were no other cars in sight, nor did he see any pedestrians. Thankful for this stroke of luck, he breathed a sigh of relief and sped away. The judge later read in the papers that the boy had suffered multiple fractures but was expected to fully recover. He also noted that all the boy could say about the car that hit him was that it was large and black. Calvert resolved to make amends by harshly sentencing the next few hit-and-run drivers that came before him. He briefly considered sending money to the boy's family for his care, but decided against it. The boy would be taken of, if not by insurance, than by one of Harbor City's charities.

However, there had been a witness. A secretary who worked at the office building in front of where the accident had occurred. She had been standing in the doorway of the side entrance, enjoying a last minute smoke. Her boss was a doctor, and did not permit smoking in his office. As she was taking her last puff, she heard the sounds of metal hitting flesh, and looked out in time to see the boy hit the sidewalk and the judge speed away. She recognized Calvert from the pictures she had seen of him in the newspapers' society pages. Concealed by the shadows of the doorway, she had not been visible to the judge.

Calvert learned of this witness two days after the accident when she called his chambers. Since he had not yet come forward, she was calling to give him a chance "to do the right thing." If he did not, then she would go to the police. He was to call her with his decision. She gave him the number of the doctor's office where she worked. When Calvert asked her how much she wanted to forget what she had seen, she hung up on him.

Looking back just before the end, Calvert decided that he really should have heeded her advice and turned himself in. He should not have made a deal with William Brody, a repeat offender whom Calvert was to sentence on an assault charge. In exchange for making his problem with the secretary "go away," Calvert offered to make sure that Brody not serve any time for the assault. The deal was struck only when the judge offered money as an additional reward. Calvert reminded Brody to make sure there were no witnesses to whatever he had to do to insure the woman's silence.

Brody took the judge at his word. When he was finished, the doctor's secretary was dead, shot to death in the office where she worked. The doctor was also dead, as was anyone who may have seen Brody's face. When William Brody walked out of the Hamilton Medical Center, he left behind twelve bodies. There was no one who could identify him.

Calvert first learned of the massacre when he read about it in the morning papers. When he saw the headlines, he was no more appalled than any citizen of Harbor City. This was a violent town, and these things happen. Then he read where the killings had taken place and realized what he had done.

As he read the article, the judge next grew angry. How could any human being be that stupid? *Serves me right, hiring an amateur,* Calvert thought. *I should have called Pratt or one of the other gang bosses. There would have been favor for favor, but I could have lived with that.*

A brief moment of worry then passed through Calvert's mind. It passed when he read that the gunman had gotten away and that the police, as usual, had no leads as to his identity. And what if he were caught? A man who kills twelve people is obviously unstable.

"Why did he say that you hired him, Your Honor?" Calvert rehearsed in his mind.

"Who can say? I did the man a good turn, gave him a break in court. Maybe he saw that as sign to go out and start killing. Who knows with these sick people?" Yes, that would work.

Calvert's next surprise came the following day when the Devil came to call.

Harbor City was a crime-plagued town. It was ruled by a number of competing gangs, all of whom had their contacts and employees in City Hall, the District Attorney's office and the courts. The only really honest agency in the city was the police department, thanks largely to the efforts of the police commissioner and the good people he had hired. Faced with ever increasing crime and out of control gang activity, the Commissioner had appointed Sergeant Frank Devlin to a special detail. Devlin was to go after those gangsters, who, for whatever reason, had managed to place themselves beyond the law. He had succeeded admirably. In only six months, Devlin had killed two gang leaders, stopped two gang wars, and had dispatched a number of minor crooks protected by the corrupt system of Harbor City justice. So effective was he that he had earned the nickname "the Devil."

Calvert had never had much to do with the gangs. By Harbor City standards his hands were clean. Yes, there had been the occasional financial inducement to disallow this evidence or grant parole to that defendant, but he had never taken money or accepted favors in deciding major cases. Gambling, drugs and loansharking were one thing. The occasional armed robbery without actual violence, maybe. Cases involving murder, mayhem, and rape were not for sale. Of course, Judge Calvert never raised any objection when such cases were transferred from his court to that of a judge with a stronger connection to one of the mob lords.

The Devil came at an inopportune moment. The judge was enjoying the affections of a pretty young law student when his clerk interrupted. Calvert had her promise to meet him after the afternoon session and admitted Devlin. That's when things got better - and worse.

Brody had been identified, not by witnesses but by fingerprints. (*Gloves*, thought Calvert, *haven't these crooks ever heard about gloves?*) Worse yet, one of the victims was the aunt of Louis Martinelli, another of the gang leaders who ruled Harbor City. Martinelli was of the old school. As a matter of honor, he would personally lead a hunt for his aunt's killers and, once found, they would be no more. And, unlike the court system, Martinelli could not be bought off. That was the bad news.

Devlin questioned the judge as to his reasons for giving Brody a light sentence on the assault charge. He wanted to know if Calvert had been offered any "inducement" to do so. Feigning indignation, Calvert vehemently denied the charge. Inwardly, he was thankful that there was no other indication that he and Brody were connected.

Devlin seemed satisfied with Calvert's answers to his questions. After Devlin left, the judge was much happier than when he had arrived. With Devlin on the case, Brody would most likely not live to testify. The encounter between Brody and the Devil would be short, violent, and fatal. The law, and Martinelli, would be satisfied, and Calvert would remain free and uninvolved.

The next morning, Calvert read of Brody's death at the hands of the Devil. His problems were over. He did not expect any more trouble.

He certainly did not expect The Devil to barge into his courtroom and publicly accuse him of being responsible for the murders. Neither did he expect Devlin to produce the witness to his hit-and run, the witness that Brody was to have killed. And he certainly did not expect to learn that Brody had killed the wrong secretary. The women who had seen the accident had been merely a fill-in. The doctor's regular secretary had been on vacation, and returned to work the very day that Brody struck. She had died instead.

The press had been in the courtroom, invited by Devlin. They had eagerly filled notebooks and snapped photos as Devlin mounted the bench in Calvert's place and proclaimed his guilt for all, and especially Martinelli, to hear.

It was now late in the evening. Those who had not seen the afternoon papers had surely read the story in the evening editions. By now, Martinelli would have made his plans regarding Calvert's fate. The judge had been making his own plans, or at least, trying to.

To his credit, Calvert first called his wife. It took him some time to get through to his house.

"Steven, are you all right? Reporters have been calling here for the last hour wanting to know about you and some secretary's murder. What happened today?"

"Marie, listen. There was some trouble in court today. There's more coming."

"But, what kind of trouble?"

"I don't want to explain now, I can't really. Just take the boys and go."

"Go where? Steven, are we in danger?"

"I don't think so." That was the truth, or so he hoped. Martinelli considered himself a man of honor. He did not make war on innocents or family. He took out his vengeance only on those who deserved it. However, Calvert did not want to take any chances. His own actions had resulted in the death of a member of Martinelli's family. He might just decide to pay Calvert back in his own coin.

"Marie, there's a lot happening now that I can't explain. It would be best if you and the boys were out of the city. Take the emergency cash and go. Don't tell anyone where you're going, or even that you're leaving. Just go."

"Should I call you when I get someplace?" Calvert could hear the worry in her voice. She was controlling it, for the sake of the boys, he guessed. He almost said "Yes," just so he'd hear her voice one more time.

"No, don't call." It was not beyond Martinelli to be able to somehow listen in on his phone calls, however difficult that was to do. "Don't call," he repeated.

"How will I know when to come back?"

For the first time, Calvert realized the sentence he was under. He would try to avoid it, might even be able to delay it for a time, but in the end . . .

"Steven, are you still there?"

"Yes. Marie, wherever you stop, make sure that you can get the Harbor City papers. Just read the papers, you'll know when to come back."

"Steven . . ."

"Marie, listen. I have to go soon. Just remember, whatever happens, whatever has happened, I've always loved you." He hung up, and prayed that she'd follow his instructions.

He sat awhile in his chambers, thinking about how much he had given up just to pursue what he now saw as idle pleasures. He had never thought he'd get caught, and he never planned for the sequence of events that his adultery had caused.

His next phone calls were to Harbor City's shadow lords. Calling Martinelli was out, unless he wanted to surrender and accept a quick death. Anthony Peterson was out of town, had been for some time. It was commonly believed that he was either in hiding or else would eventually turn up in the trunk of an abandoned car. Calvert personally believed the former story. From all that he had heard, Peterson's gang was still together, still running smoothly. Peterson was probably running things from a safe distance.

That left Jonas Lombardi and Harry Pratt as the only gang leaders strong enough to stand against Martinelli. The judge called Lombardi first.

"Judge Calvert, what a surprise, nice of you to call." The judge could tell that, however pleased the mob boss had been to hear from him, his call had not been a surprise. There was a kind of humor tinged with malice in Lombardi's voice, the tone that you use upon hearing that something unfortunate has happened to someone who truly deserved it.

"How can I help you, Your Honor? Wait, let me guess. You need somebody to protect you from Martinelli, right?"

"You've heard."

"Yeah, I heard. One of the Globe's reporters gave me a call just after Judge Devil passed sentence on you. You know, you really should have called me sooner. You wouldn't be in the fix you're in. But then, you never really wanted much to do with us, anyway, did you?"

"Is there anyway you can help me?"

"Calvert, let me tell you. First of all, I don't owe you anything. Everything you did for us, and it wasn't much, was paid for in advance. Next, you got nothing to bargain with. Tomorrow, the day after, you're not a judge anymore, so you're no good to me. Finally, there's no way I'm crossing Martinelli. He may not have the biggest outfit in this city, but when he wants something done, it gets done, and so does whoever gets in his way. It's like your new best friend Devlin says, 'It's time to pay for your sins.' Sorry, Calvert." Lombardi broke the connection.

Calvert listened to the dial tone for a long time, then called Harry Pratt. He got much the same answer. There was one other call he could make. He'd call the Commissioner and turn himself in, confess to hiring Brody. He'd be in jail, but he'd still be alive.

For how long? came the sudden thought. The Devil was the Commissioner's own weapon. He had probably sent Devlin. Why would he agree to help after setting him up to be killed? And Martinelli would be able to reach him as easily in jail as he could on the outside, even if the judge could arrange protective custody. Calvert quietly contemplated life in jail. Life? He'd been responsible for the deaths of twelve people. He'd spend what life he had left on death row, waiting to ride the lightning to an unmarked grave.

There was nothing to do. He was not equipped for a life on the run. He had no extra cash put away, beyond what his wife was taking. Neither did he have the skills to live on the rough. Judge Calvert sat back in his chair. Here was as good a place as any to wait. Sooner or later someone would come for him. Then, at least, it would be over.

It was late afternoon when a uniformed guard knocked on the door and entered without waiting. As the door opened, Calvert could hear the sounds of the courthouse personnel getting ready to leave for the day.

"Your Honor." Calvert looked up. "I've been sent to take you home. The chief judge thought it best to wait until everyone else was leaving, less chance of your being seen that way."

Maybe he did have a chance. "Not home, officer. Take me to a hotel. I'll check in under a different name, maybe I'll figure out what to do tomorrow."

The guard nodded and escorted him to the garage under the courthouse. He led the judge to an unmarked car, explaining that anyone watching would be looking for Calvert's car as well. As he got into the front of the late model sedan, he saw another figure sitting in the back, the poor lighting of garage having hidden him until now.

"You're not taking me to a hotel, are you?" Calvert asked the guard, who had settled himself behind the wheel.

Staring straight ahead, the guard answered, "No, I'm not." He turned on the ignition, but before putting the car in gear, turned to the judge. "Judge, you can probably guess what's coming, but if you give us any trouble, it'll come a lot sooner and be a lot messier. So just sit back and try to enjoy whatever time you've got left."

Benjamin Campbell was tired of waiting. Ever since he and that crazy Devlin had left the courtroom he had been staked out in front of the Hamilton Medical Building. At first, he sat in a borrowed taxi, pretending to be waiting for a fare. After it grew dark, he switched to a plain looking sedan. He had it parked so that it was not too obvious from the street, yet afforded a view of the front steps of the medical building. He was waiting for a judge.

Campbell was a sergeant with the Harbor City Police department. He was assigned to the Homicide Squad, and a few days ago it had been his job to investigate the massacre at the building he was now watching. He had just started when Devlin showed up.

He liked Devlin from the start. The guy had a hard job, being the Commissioner's special agent. Campbell had only shot one man in his life. He hadn't even killed him, yet he had felt bad about it for days. He'd even considered quitting the force. He could only imagine what Devlin had been going through. The man everyone called "The Devil" must have killed over twenty men by now. So when Devlin appeared on the crime scene Campbell did the only thing a decent guy could do for another cop who needed a lift, he'd joked with him about it. Devlin responded in kind, and the two worked well together.

They worked together well enough to come up with Brody as the shooter, even if Devlin had to go and kill him before Brody named the man who hired him. Even then, the two had put their heads together and identified Judge Calvert as the man behind Brody. Then Devlin had to pull another one of his Devil stunts and accuse Calvert in open court. What had started as a scheme to get Calvert to confess quickly became a circus, ending with Calvert fleeing the bench and Devlin all but giving Louis Martinelli an open invitation to kill the judge.

Which is why Campbell was waiting outside the medical building. It had been his experience that gangsters, especially ones who had a point to make, went in for dramatic gestures. He fully expected Martinelli to have Calvert's body dumped on the front steps on the Hamilton. He wanted to be there when it was.

He almost asked Devlin to join him in the stake out. He quickly reconsidered when he realized that he wanted live witnesses and not more dead gunmen. Besides, Devlin had seemed content to let Martinelli have a pass on this one.

Campbell's thoughts were interrupted when he noticed a car slowly driving down Church Street. The car rolled to a stop in front of the main entrance to the medical center, the doors of which were still boarded over from Brody's shooting through them. Campbell slumped lower in his seat as the driver of the other car looked around. Satisfied that no one was watching him, the driver gave a nod to the man in the back seat. From his viewpoint across the street, Campbell could see the back door open and the man in the back give something a shove. Campbell used his car's radio to give an order to his waiting men. He hoped that his guess was right. He'd be very embarrassed if they were just two men dumping garbage.

Coming from alleys, pulling out of parking spaces, driving the opposite directions on one- way streets, Campbell's men closed the trap. With their sirens screaming, the unmarked radio cars converged on the area. Campbell had deployed them so that all possible routes of escape were blocked off. The car in front of the medical center started to move away from the curb, but stopped after traveling just a few feet. The passenger in the rear very carefully locked his hands behind his head. The driver was just as careful not to remove his hands from the steering wheel. Neither man was certain that the Devil was not among all those cops.

As Campbell approached the car, he heard the one in the back tell the driver, "Just remember, everything's going to be all right."

"I'll try, but we got a dozen cops out there all waiting for us to move funny."

"Hey, quiet, here comes somebody."

"It ain't Devlin, is it?" the driver asked nervously.

"Nah, it's just some homicide cop. I seen him before."

"Good, then we might live through this."

Gun drawn, Campbell walked over to the car and peered in, just to see if he recognized its riders. Eddie Stefano and Joey Prestone, two of Martinelli's soldiers, looked back at him and tried to smile. The driver, Stefano, said with as much innocence as he could muster, "Is there a problem, Officer?"

Campbell straightened up and walked around the car to look at what they had pushed onto the sidewalk. It was with some relief that he saw a body lying on the concrete. Any guilt that he felt about that faded when he made sure that the deceased was indeed Judge Steven Calvert. Calvert would have died anyway, and whether he was killed by the state or by Martinelli made little difference to the detective. At least this way, it gave the police a shot at Martinelli.

Which was probably Devlin's plan all along, Campbell suddenly thought. He looked around to see if the Devil was standing somewhere in the darkness.

No, he dismissed that idea. That was what those guys in New York used to do. Devlin's not one to play with shadows.

Campbell tapped on the back glass of the car and motioned for Prestone to lower his window.

"There's a fine for littering in this city." He pointed to the body with his gun.

"I'm sorry, Officer. Can we just pay the ticket and go?"

The detective shook his head and waved the patrol wagon over. Martinelli's two gunmen were handcuffed and put in the back.

"Downtown with them," Campbell told the driver. "The desk sergeant already knows where to put them."

During the ride downtown, a worried Stefano asked Prestone, "We're going to be okay, right Joey?"

"Listen, Eddie, we were told this might happen. Remember, Martinelli's promised to take care of everything. We just have to stay calm, and not give anything away. The boss ain't ever gone back on his word yet."

Once downtown, the two were immediately separated. Each soon found himself in a small room, sitting at a table. One wrist was locked into a handcuff that was bolted right onto the table's surface. The chair on the other side of the table was empty. Both men waited.

Stefano did not know how long he had been watching the door, waiting for someone to come in. They had taken his watch, and all other property, at the desk when he came in. Finally, the door opened and Campbell came in and sat in the chair across from him.

"Evening, Eddie." Stefano just nodded in reply.

"Eddie, I'm hoping you and me can win a little bet that I've got with another officer."

"What's that?" Stefano asked. This was not starting off like any other interrogation that he had been through.

"You see, Eddie, Sergeant Devlin and I have a disagreement about the correct way to question homicide suspects. I believe that if you politely ask them for information, they'll gladly tell you whatever it is you want to know. Sergeant Devlin believes otherwise. So we made a bet. The winner is whoever gets his suspect to talk first."

"If I can ask, Sergeant, what does the Dev... I mean, Sergeant Devlin believe?"

As if in answer, there came a sound from the next room. Stefano had heard that sound before, had made that sound himself many times, in working for Martinelli and other gang bosses. It was the sound of a heavy pipe hitting a telephone book. It was the sound of a large bag of flour falling off the shelf onto the ground. It was the sound of one human being methodically beating another.

"As I said, Eddie, Sergeant Devlin has his own ideas about questioning prisoners."

Stefano was torn between feeling sorry for what Joey was going through and relief that he had drawn Campbell and not Devlin. He was also glad that he would not be the one to rat out Martinelli. He'd listen to Campbell's polite questions and simply not answer.

"About the bet, Eddie," Campbell waited until he had the prisoner's full attention. "The winner gets to question the loser's prisoner."

As the noise from the next room continued, Campbell let the gunman listen for a minute or so, then he started asking questions. Stefano told him exactly what he wanted to hear.

A half-hour after Campbell entered Interrogation Room 1, he left with the evidence he needed to lock up one of Harbor City's top gang leaders. He hoped that his associate had had as much luck with the other prisoner. The sounds of a savage beating were still coming from Room 2 as the door to the third room opened and Detective Waynesboro came out.

"How did it go?" Campbell asked the detective.

"Just like you said it would. I started asking him the questions you gave me just after the, um, beating started, and he opened right up."

"He give up Martinelli?"

"He would have given up the mayor, pope, and president when he heard what was going on next door."

Both men laughed, and Campbell opened the door to Room 2.

"You can stop now," he told the officer who was beating on a sack of flour with his nightstick.

"Did it work?" the officer asked. His face and uniform were white from his powdery assault, at his feet were two more bags of flour, split open from his efforts.

At Campbell's nod, he smiled and added, "The next time, Sarge, could we use a phone book?"

About the same time that Campbell was setting up for his stakeout, Frank Devlin was making his report to the Commissioner of Harbor City's Police Department. A frown that was already on the Commissioner's face deepened when Devlin got to the part where he ascended to the judge's bench and passed judgement on the Honorable Steven Calvert.

While making his report, Devlin got the feeling that the Commissioner knew all about what had happened in the courtroom. The afternoon edition of the Globe would be out by now, and the Chief would have received his copy.

After he finished his report, Devlin sat back in his chair and prepared himself for the chewing out he was sure was coming. He was not disappointed.

"Sergeant Devlin," This was bad. The Commissioner only used both his surname and rank under the most formal or serious circumstances. "Just what the Hell were you thinking?"

Devlin started to defend his actions but his boss cut him off. "Never mind, from this evening's papers and what you just told me it's quite clear that you weren't thinking." The Commissioner read from the papers that were on his desk.

"This afternoon's Globe - 'Justice Goes to Hell.' This evening's Post - 'His Honor, the Devil.' And my personal favorite, an extra The Sun put out."

"I thought The Sun was a morning paper."

"For you, Sergeant, they made an exception."

The Chief held up the last mentioned paper. The front page carried the same photograph as the others, that of Devlin seated at the judge's bench. In larger than usual type, the headline above the picture read, "Judge, Jury . . ." It finished below the photo, "And Executioner?"

"If case you were wondering, Sergeant, it speculates on how long Judge Calvert has left to live. It gives him no more than 48 hours." The Commissioner opened the paper and turned to the back page. "The editorial suggests that the city could save quite a bit of money by closing the D.A.'s office and shutting down the courts. It suggests that you be given full authority in these matters. I think the cartoon catches your likeness rather well." He held it up for Devlin to see.

The drawing showed a classic devil - horns, tail and all - with Devlin's face. He was sitting behind a judge's bench, and was blowing smoke from the barrel of a .38. In the background was a bailiff holding a three-headed dog by a leash. Lying in front of the bench were several bullet-ridden bodies. The caption had the devil saying, "Next case."

"And now, Sergeant, now that you have held yourself, me and everyone in this department up to public ridicule, would you care to explain yourself?"

"Well, Sir, it seemed like a good idea at the time."

"So did Prohibition."

"Commissioner, first of all let me say that this was solely my idea, Sergeant Campbell was against it, but I talked him into it. He certainly had no idea that I was going to mount the bench."

"So noted, Sergeant, but Campbell is not my special deputy. Campbell does not have the hopes of many law-abiding citizens riding on his every action. Campbell did not just throw away months of very good work for a very stupid stunt."

Devlin waited until he was sure that the chief was finished. "Actually, Sir, I had no idea that I was going to mount the bench until it happened. After we identified Brody's actual target and learned who had wanted her dead, Sergeant Campbell and I both realized that there was no way we could bring Calvert to justice."

"Thanks to your killing Brody. You just covered yourself in glory in this case, didn't you?"

Devlin decided that silence was the safest reply. After allowing a moment to pass to acknowledge the reprimand, he continued.

"We were sure that the judge had ordered the killing. I had hoped to surprise a confession out of him by confronting him in the place he felt the safest, his courtroom. Failing that, I'd expose him in public, that's why the press was there. At least there'd be some justice."

"Even if Martinelli delivered it?"

"Yes, Sir. You told me when all this started to do whatever it takes to bring down those beyond the law. In this case, that meant using a ganglord to avenge innocent people."

The Commissioner thought about this last comment. He had given Devlin almost full rein and had placed no limits on his activities. "So, it's all my fault?"

"No, sir, I take full responsibility for my actions."

"So do we all, son, so do we all, and you operate under my authority, so I bear part of that responsibility. Just tell me, Frank, why did you take the bench?"

Devlin breathed an inward sigh of relief. The Commissioner's use of his first name meant that he was at least partially forgiven, and that the session was almost over.

"It was a spur of the moment decision. I had meant only to act the part of a prosecutor, but when Calvert tried to leave, I was caught up in the drama of the situation, and next I knew, I was on the bench pronouncing judgement."

"Sergeant, for the record you should know that the mayor and two of Calvert's fellow jurists have called my office and demanded, if not your resignation, then at least a healthy suspension. Mr. Szold called and suggested that, if Calvert is killed, Internal Affairs might investigate you as an accomplice to his death. And, finally, I'm not too sure that this whole 'Devil' business hasn't gotten out of hand."

The Commissioner paused, shook his head, then finally added, "Go home, Frank, we'll talk later. There are calls I have to make, and then I have to think about this whole thing."

Devlin stood up at his dismissal. "Sir?"

"Yes, Sergeant?"

"If I may ask, the mayor and those two judges, what did you tell them?"

"I told them that you might be an idiot, but you're *my* idiot and they're stuck with both of us. Good night, Sergeant."

"Good night, Sir."

It was just after eight in the evening. Devlin was at home, trying to read. Worry about what the Commissioner might decide about his assignment kept him from enjoying his book. Could he go back to regular police work after being the Devil? Would the press or the mobs let him "retire" that easily? It would be a relief in a way, to be just Frank Devlin, and not have to worry about living up to the reputation his nickname had given him.

What good was he doing? He'd killed some men who deserved it, brought them to a justice they otherwise would have never met. Others took their place and he hunted them down too. So much killing. Every night he prayed that he'd never grow numb to it. Still, the job needed to be done, and he had agreed to do it. He only wished he knew how to do it better.

He gave up trying to read and turned on the television, hoping to find a variety show to distract him. Then the phone rang. It was the Commissioner.

"Campbell just called. Calvert's dead. Be in my office first thing tomorrow." Devlin acknowledged the order and his boss hung up.

IV

Before reporting to headquarters the next morning, Devlin read what the morning papers had to say about his courtroom activities and the judge's death. Neither of the two dailys were as kind to him as the previous day's papers had been. The Sun ran its same headline, changing the question mark to an exclamation point. It also ran a photograph of Judge Calvert's dead body on the sidewalk directly under the word "Executioner." A front-page editorial called for an investigation of Devlin's entire career as the

Devil.

The Mob-controlled Sentinel was worse. This tabloid called for Devlin's immediate imprisonment and indictment as the probable killer of Judge Calvert, suggesting that he had framed the judge and planned to pin the blame for his murder on "honest businessmen."

Devlin usually walked to work. This morning, anticipating a crowd of newsmen lying in wait outside of headquarters, he took a cab to the rear garage entrance, warning the cabby not to alert his dispatcher about whom he was carrying.

"A quick twenty from the Post is not worth the loss of your hack license." The cabby agreed. Jobs in Harbor City were scarce that year.

During the cab ride, Devlin wondered what it was about the newspaper stories that was bothering him. He had expected Martinelli to act against the man responsible for his aunt's death, and Devlin's public accusation had called for a public response. The dumping of the body as described in the papers, however, did not seem to be Martinelli's style. Seldom had the gang boss sought the limelight in the way his fellow mobsters had. Devlin had expected Martinelli to let the judge worry for a time, then strike shortly after Calvert let down his guard. The judge should have disappeared, with no body and nothing to trace back to his killer. If the papers had it right, this execution was sloppily done.

Still, Martinelli was not above teaching more than one lesson at once. Devlin had put Martinelli on the spot, using him as a weapon of justice. The public disposal of Calvert's body, coming so soon after Devlin had been blasted in the afternoon papers, could have been Martinelli's way of adding to Devlin's problems. Martinelli did not like to be used.

The cab pulled up to the garage entrance. Devlin showed his badge and the taxi was allowed in as far as the visitors' parking. Devlin paid the fare and added a healthy tip.

"Thanks, Devil, and hey, listen, don't worry about what those rags print about you. It's about time somebody went after the big shots. This city stinks from the head down and just taking out the little guys don't help. You keep doing what you gotta do, even if you gotta fight City Hall, know what I mean?" The cabby turned his thumb and index finger into a pistol to make sure Devlin got the message.

"I know what you mean, friend, and thanks. First kind words I've heard in days."

Devlin was to hear more kind words that day. On going up to the Commissioner's office, he was lead right in. The Chief motioned him to take his seat and started talking before Devlin could sit down.

"You've seen this morning's papers?" Without waiting for a reply he went on. "Don't worry about them. Next time you take down a gang leader or kill a bank robber you'll be a hero again. This," the Chief held up The Sun, "comes with the job."

"You didn't think so yesterday."

"Yesterday you needed a chewing out. Today, well, things have changed. Michael …"

A man stepped out of the shadows in the far corner of the room, behind and to the left of the Commissioner's desk. Being familiar with the office, Devlin had sensed his presence, but had said nothing, figuring that his boss had his reasons for what he did.

"Frank, this is Michael Shaw, he's been doing some work for me."

Shaw pulled up a chair and sat at the end of the desk, completing a triangle with the other men.

"What kind of work?" Devlin asked, leaving it up to either of the other two to answer.

"Frank," answered the Chief, "You remember my telling you that one of your jobs was to keep the mobs busy. That you were to divert their attention from other investigations. Well, Michael is part of those other investigations. Fill Devlin in, Michael."

"First of all, Sergeant, let me say that I've been following your career with great interest, and I'm quite impressed. However, let me, as your boss said, fill you in.

"I run a very private investigation agency out of New York. About the time you traded your tin badge for a gold one, the Commissioner called me in to do some undercover work in the courts and D.A.'s office. With help from the chief judge and the D.A. himself, I put my people into some low-level positions - janitors, maintenance, secretarial. They've managed to learn enough to direct further inquires. The next step will be to introduce additional agents as new court clerks, recorders, and prosecutors. These people will allow themselves to be seduced by the easy money that can be had by taking lesser pleas, losing evidence, arranging schedules so that the 'right' judges get the "right' cases and the like. We may even bring in a new judge. I understand there's an opening."

The jest was so unexpected and so well delivered that the other two men had to chuckle. Shaw joined in on his own joke, then continued, "Once we learn where the money's coming from, we'll investigate further, applying the needed pressure to learn who else is taking it. That's where you'll come in, Sergeant."

"How so?"

"They'll talk to us, or . . ." Shaw paused to make his meaning quite clear, "Or they'll pay for their sins."

Devlin started as he heard his usual warning thrown back at him. Did he really sound like that? Coming from Shaw, it was a death sentence.

"Given that choice, they'll talk." The Commissioner went on to explain how Campbell got his confessions of the night before, and that right now an indictment was being prepared against Martinelli.

"So that's the first bit of good news, one more boss down. We may never catch him, but we can close down his restaurant and lock up most of his known people as material witnesses. He can't show his face, he can't make a move, he's out of business. Tell him the other good news, Michael."

"Your little performance had unexpected side effects, Sergeant.

Even as early as yesterday afternoon, the word at court was that you were targeting judges, lawyers, etc. A few have already been overheard discussing curtailing their activities or even turning themselves in. It seems that no one wants to deal with the Devil."

"That should make it easier for your people when you put them in."

"Exactly, Sergeant. And finally, something from New York for you. It seems that your Tony Peterson has been seen in my hometown trying to recruit some talent."

"Seen where? The NYPD hasn't reported anything on him."

"They wouldn't. Peterson has been asking about gunmen at places like The Junction and Dago Mike's, places the police don't dare go."

"But your people do," asked Devlin, suddenly more impressed by this Micahel Shaw.

Shaw nodded, then added, "A word of warning, Sergeant. Some of the men that Peterson has been seen talking to are quite formidable, not the type to be easily impressed by a small town cop with a fancy nickname."

"Small town?"

"To New Yorkers, anywhere else is a small town."

"These men, Mr. Shaw, could you handle them?"

"Once maybe, Sergeant, but I'm done with that now."

The Devil let the obvious false modesty slide. "Let them come, Mr. Shaw. They'll learn that every small town has a Boot Hill."

V

Prestone and Stefano had been taken from the police lock-up to the holding cells in the basement of the courthouse. Tomorrow, they would plea guilty to an accessory charge in exchange for a much-reduced sentence. Their sworn statements, already given to Campbell, that Martinelli had personally ordered Calvert to be killed would be read into the record. Neither man was worried. They had been assured that the boss had covered everything, and, if it came to a trial, they were both prepared to swear that, no, Martinelli did not give them the order, but that was what they had been told. It wasn't their fault that the detectives had asked the wrong questions.

When they got to the holding cells, a guard was waiting to take them in charge. He led them to an isolated cellblock, where informants and material witnesses were usually kept. He closed the cell doors behind them, then drew his weapon.

Stefano wondered why the guard would draw his gun with both of them safely locked up. Then he noticed that the weapon was an automatic, and not the standard issue .38.

"The boss wants to thank you boys for doing such a good job," the guard said. Prestone looked up from his cot, and Stefano thought he knew what was happening - it was a break. But why lock them up in the first place? The guard reached into his pocket, and pulled out a long tube. He screwed the silencer onto the barrel of his weapon and waited until both men understood their situation. They had nowhere to run and no place to hide, and he quietly shot them dead. He wiped the gun and threw it into the cell. His way out had been prepared, and he quickly left the building.

The restaurant was closed. The waiters had gone home for the night. The busboys had cleaned the dining room, put the chairs up and were waiting to be dismissed. The kitchen was spotless, and the cooks were now planning the next day's specials. On the surface, everything was business as usual at Martinelli's.

Except that from seven o'clock to closing, two men had sat in the dining room, picking at their manicotti. They ordered endless cups of coffee while pretending not to be policemen. Customers and busboys had reported people lurking in the shadows both by the front and back doors, more police no doubt. And Nicholas was more than busy, since, for the first time in three years, Louis Martinelli was not there to personally oversee things.

Louis Martinelli was not a stupid man, nor was he vain enough to assume that his intelligence could carry him through any crisis. He had a well-trained staff, and a smooth running operation. He had always known that one day he might be forced to take an unexpected vacation and had planned accordingly.

Martinelli had read of the confrontation between Devlin and Judge Calvert, and of the Devil's challenge to him. When he learned of the judge's death, he knew what had to be done. He left notes for his daughter and Nicholas and left quietly, without a word to anyone but his driver and bodyguard. He'd be back when he could. He did not expect to be away long.

To regular customers, Nicholas was just the restaurant's maitre d'. To others, he was that and much more. He would handle the daily operations of serving customers and seeing that the food was properly prepared and presented. Angela could handle the business end. Why else had the boss sent her to all those fancy schools? Nicholas also expected to hear from his boss from time to time, arrangements had been made in advance, and was prepared to handle any special assignments given him.

Having dismissed the busboys, Nicholas sat alone in the quiet darkness of the dining room. He could hear the cooks arguing about tomorrow's menu and the clicks of Angela's adding machine. As worried as she was about her father, she would at least be pleased by tonight's receipts.

Martinelli's had been more than crowded. Lines had formed early, as soon as the evening papers had reported the boss's possible indictment. People were attracted to the false allure of crime, and this was good for business. Nicholas wondered how long it would last, before some other event chased this story off the front pages, or before the authorities moved to seize Martinelli's assets. Nicholas chuckled. They'd be surprised when they learned that the boss, at least on paper, did not own his own restaurant. Whatever else happened, Martinelli's would stay open.

Nicholas's enjoyment of the quiet was broken by shouts from the kitchen. He rushed back, hoping not to find to cooks facing each other with knives again.

He and Angela reached the kitchen at the same time. The cooks did have knives in their hands, but they were facing the rear exit. Standing in the doorway, the door behind him shut to avoid being framed by the light of the kitchen, was the Devil.

"We have to talk," Devlin said, and without opposition, he walked straight to Martinelli's private dining room, leaving Nicholas and Angela to follow if they would.

Devlin was seated at Martinelli's table when Angela joined him. He sat off to the side, motioning to Angela to take the center chair. Nicholas soon joined them with a bottle of wine and three glasses.

As Nicholas poured, Angela looked at Devlin and asked, "Tell me, why should I be drinking with my father's enemy?"

Devlin waited for the wine to be poured, then took a healthy sip before answering. This gave him time to again study Martinelli's daughter.

Angela Martinelli looked nothing like her father. Instead, with her red hair, green eyes, and a bridge of freckles across her nose, she was more like her Irish mother. Devlin remembered that some ten years ago, Bridget Martinelli had returned to Dublin, unable to reconcile her upbringing with her husband's profession. She had taken Angela with her. Martinelli allowed this, reasoning that his daughter was safer in Ireland than on the streets of Harbor City. Besides, a girl's place was with her mother.

But such a life with her mother had been too restrictive for the daughter of Louis Martinelli. When Angela was eighteen, she returned home. Martinelli sent her to the best schools, and in the summer she stayed home and learned what she could of her father's business. She may have her mother's looks, but she had her father's temperament and talents.

Swallowing his wine, Devlin turned her way.

"Miss Martinelli, your father is not my enemy. True, we are on opposite sides, but he has not done anything to merit my special attention. We have, in fact, done each other favors in the past."

"Sergeant," Nicholas said quietly, "If you are here to search for Mr. Martinelli, I can tell you that he is not present. You are, of course, welcome to check the entire building, but it would be a waste of your time and ours."

"Nicholas, Miss Martinelli, I am not here to either look for or arrest anyone."

"Then why have the police surrounded the house?"

"They are not my men, Miss, and I had quite a time in avoiding them myself. As I said, we have to talk."

"Sergeant Devlin, there is nothing to talk about. You first drag my father's name out in public, and invite him to kill a judge, as if he would. He had plans to deal with whoever gave the orders that killed our aunt, and they did not include a public execution. You next coerce a confession from two men whose loyalties change at the flash of money or threat of violence. You will charge my father with murder, and kill him if you can. Tell me, what have we to talk about?"

"Your father didn't do it, or have it done."

Neither of the other two at the table had anything to say at Devlin's pronouncement. Taking advantage of the silence, he went on.

"True, I did invite Martinelli to arrange his own justice for Calvert, but I did not expect a public execution. Your father has always done things with a certain style. The judge would have disappeared for a time, and would then have probably returned a much chastened man, eternally beholden to Martinelli. It was not like your father to waste such a resource. And if your father did decide that Calvert was not fit to live, than that was so much justice and I'm sure that the body would never have been found."

Devlin caught Nicholas nodding at this last statement, and continued.

"So this made me suspicious. I read the transcripts of the questioning of the men who dumped the judge. They were asked if Martinelli had been involved, and if he had given the order to kill Calvert. As they were under some inducement to tell their interrogators what they wanted to hear, they quickly agreed, and gave sworn statements to that effect."

"They are dead men." Nicholas uttered this threat with no regard for the detective sitting across the table from him.

"More than you know." Devlin explained that the bodies of the two men were found in their cell not long ago.

"Their deaths convinced me. With them dead, their statements can be used against Martinelli in court. Alive, they could always be convinced to change their testimony in court. I'm sure that your father had some means of convincing them." Devlin looked pointedly at Nicholas. The man who was much more than a maitre d' nodded his head in reply to the unasked question. "Martinelli would not have had them killed, not yet anyway. So someone else did."

"Which convinces you that someone else killed Calvert, leaving Mr. Martinelli to take the blame."

"Exactly, Nicholas, but who?" Devlin could have answered his own question, but he was working up to something.

"You know, you know who this man is?"

"Not yet, Miss Martinelli, but I know who to ask."

Devlin took a sip of wine before continuing. "Think for a minute. Who could use two of your men and make them think that Martinelli gave the order? Who has the skills and contacts to arrange for a hit inside the courthouse? And finally," Devlin paused to break the news gradually, "Who knew where your father might be hiding?"

"Why is this important?" Angela asked, worried by the look on Devlin's face.

"Because the State Police arrested your father this afternoon. They found him in a cabin in the western mountains. He'll be brought back for arraignment tomorrow."

"That's impossible!" Angela abruptly stood up, turned and confronted Devlin. "No one knew where my father was going. He told no one."

"Except his bodyguard and chauffeur." Nicholas added quietly.

He had seen Angela mad before, and did not want to be the focus of her anger.

"Men who reported to ..." prompted Devlin.

"Johnny Carlow," came the answer from both Nicholas and Angela.

"So now we know who to ask," replied the Devil.

Johnny Carlow was Martinelli's top lieutenant. With Angela handling the business end, and Nicholas taking care of any "special projects" that might come up, Carlow was responsible for the daily operations. He assigned duties and supervised the outfit's soldiers. Until tonight, he had been a trusted member of the organization.

Devlin and Nicholas made their plans. They had agreed that only the two of them would pay a visit to Carlow's house. Devlin did not want to bring any other member of the police department in on his temporary alliance with Martinelli's gang. Nicholas, for his part, did not want word of a split in the organization to get out. Just as the men were ready to leave, Angela stopped them.

"What about my father?"

"What about him, Miss Angela? The boss is in the hands of the State Police. When he is brought back tomorrow, this will all be over."

"Will it, Nicholas? Can you guarantee his safety? Can you, Sergeant Devlin?"

"Miss Martinelli, short of him being here in this house, your father is safer with the State Police than anywhere else. After we see Carlow, I'll make it a point to be there when he's brought in. By that time, all charges should be dropped."

"And if they're not, he goes to jail. And soon after that he'll be able to ask Eddie and Joey what happened."

"Miss Martinelli, our only choices are to question Carlow, or free your father. The one should clear this whole matter up. The other can only lead to a confrontation with fellow officers, and additional charges against your father - us, too, for that matter."

"But what if you drove out tonight and took custody of him? He'd be safe then."

Nicholas cut in before Devlin could answer. "Miss Angela, the Devil's involvement might tip Carlow off that we know something. All would be lost. It's better our way."

"So my father takes his chances."

"He takes his chances," Devlin said flatly. "Your father chose his way of life, and that includes the risks that go with it."

Devlin nodded to Nicholas that it was time to go, more to end the argument than anything else. Devlin was not about to go against the State Police. Martinelli should be safe. The troopers would be ready for any problems.

Nicholas led the way back to the kitchen and sent some men out to cause a distraction that would draw off the police watching the restaurant.

"What will they do?" Devlin wanted to know.

"They'll walk a block or two away, then - a few gunshots, some high-pitched screams for help, the way will be clear."

"That will work?"

"It always has before."

Some screams and a few gunshots later, the two men left the house. After they were gone, Angela Martinelli made her own plans.

Devlin and Nicholas approached Carlow's house on foot, having parked a few blocks away.

"Nice house," said Devlin. "Big enough to allow for some luxuries, not too big to attract much attention."

"The boss does not like us to draw attention to ourselves."

"Good idea, any outside guards?"

Nicholas shook his head. "That would draw attention. What about your people?"

"Nicholas, if we kept watch on every gangster in Harbor City, there'd be no one to patrol the streets."

The way clear, Nicholas walked up to the front door and rang the bell. Devlin stayed off to the side, hiding in the shadows. After a time, Carlow's bodyguard, wearing only a robe and slippers, answered it.

"You know who I am?" The guard nodded. "It is important that I speak with Carlow."

The guard stepped aside to admit Nicholas. As Nicholas entered, Devlin stepped into the light, distracting the guard. As the guard reacted to Devlin's sudden appearance, Nicholas stepped behind him and struck him in the back of the head with the blackjack he had concealed in his left hand. The guard fell. Devlin entered, stepping over the prostrate body.

"He'll be all right?" Devlin asked.

"He should be, I haven't made a mistake with one of these for at least ten years." He put the sap back into the bag he was carrying.

"No fatalities, that's good."

"I didn't say that."

"Andy, who was that at the door?"

"It's me, Johnny," Nicholas answered. "We have to talk about the boss."

"It must be important for you to come at this hour." Carlow shouted down the steps. After waiting for a reply that didn't come, he shouted again, "I'll be right down. Let me get dressed. Have Andy get you a drink. Wait in the study."

"He alone up there?" whispered Devlin.

Nicholas nodded. "His wife died years ago," he answered quietly, "And he never has any women friends over." Nicholas looked up the stairs. "Not for that, anyway."

"Then what are we waiting for, let's catch him with his pants down." The Devil started up the stairs, Nicholas close behind.

Carlow had changed from his pajamas and had just put on an undershirt and pulled up his boxers when his bedroom door opened.

"Andy, what does that pain-in-the-butt want?"

"Nothing much, Johnny, just to talk."

Carlow dropped the trousers he was about to put on when he saw the Devil in the doorway. He looked over at the gun on his night table, then looked at the one in Devlin's hand. He slowly moved away from the table and sat at the foot of the bed, one hand resting on the footboard.

Before the astonished Carlow could ask, Devlin stepped into the room and allowed Nicholas to enter. Keeping his eyes on Carlow, Martinelli's man put his bag down on a dresser, and took out a flat-blade knife.

"You know, Johnny," Nicholas started walking back and forth in front of Carlow. Devlin stood off to the side to keep both men in view. "I can see why you'd want to sell the boss out. You'd gone as far as you could in our organization, pretty far, actually, all things considered. It's only natural that you'd grab at a chance to advance just a little further with someone else. What I want to know is ..."

Nicholas made a quick motion and the knife in his hand was suddenly embedded in the footboard, less than an inch away from Carlow's hand. Carlow knew not to grab for it. Not with another knife appearing in Nicholas's hand and with the Devil standing beside him with a gun.

"… who?"

Carlow made a quick decision and hoped he'd guessed right.

"I'm not saying a thing. Thanks to your friend over there, the boss is finished in this town. So are you and the princess, once Martinelli goes down for the Calvert kill."

"I think you'll talk, Johnny, sooner or later."

"Think again, Nicky. Devlin's here for some reason, but he's still a cop. He ain't going to let you hurt me."

The Devil walked over and stuck his revolver in Carlow's ear.

"Wrong again, Johnny, all I told Nicholas was that he couldn't kill you, not tonight, anyway. There's nothing to say that *we* can't hurt you."

"But you're a cop, you got rules."

With Nicholas poised to throw another knife, Devlin slowly

thumbed back the hammer. "I'm the Devil, remember? There are no rules. I could just leave and turn you over to 'Nicky.' There might be some of you left for Andy to clean up in the morning. Or I could pull this trigger and spatter your brains all over this room, no one would care."

The Devil laughed. A dark stain started spreading over the front of Carlow's boxers.

"But that wouldn't tell us what we want to know, would it, Johnny?"

Devlin grabbed the man by the shoulder, stood him up, and pushed him against a closet door.

"Question and answer time, Johnny. I'll ask the question. Every time you don't answer, or give me a wrong one, my friend gets to play circus. Ready?"

Carlow didn't answer, and a knife flew between Carlow's spread ankles and stuck in the closet door. Nicholas reached into the bag and brought out several more knives.

"I said, 'Ready?'"

This time Carlow uttered a weak "Yeah."

"Good. First question. Why didn't Stefano and Prestone give you up when they fingered Martinelli?"

Carlow hesitated and Nicholas put a knife about a foot above the first one.

"Johnny, answer the question."

"I told them not to, that Martinelli wanted all the credit, that the cops were giving him a pass on this one. 'No matter what happens,' I told them, 'Remember, the boss was in on this all by himself.'"

"See how easy that was? Now then, the big question, who put you up to it?"

"Nobody, it was my idea, I was going to take things over once Martinelli was out of the way."

The third knife went between Carlow's thighs, just brushing his left leg and the bottom of his boxers.

"Almost got him that time, didn't you?"

"Smaller target area."

"Johnny, you're not big enough to plan this by yourself. There are not enough men loyal to you. Now, before Nicholas throws another knife and gets the blade all rusty, answer the question."

Nicholas made a show of preparing to throw as Devlin said to him in a stage whisper, "Do the ears after this." The stain on Carlow's boxers got bigger.

"Lombardi, it was Lombardi who figured on using the judge to take out Martinelli."

"Then you'd run Little Italy for him, right?"

Carlow nodded, then relaxed as much as he could when Nicholas lowered his arm. Devlin walked over to Carlow and put his arm around him.

"Who pulled the trigger, Johnny? You or Lombardi?"

Carlow was beaten. Head down, he did not even look up to see if Nicholas had readied another knife.

"Lombardi had me do it. He didn't want any of Martinelli's boys to see him."

"Do you swear, Johnny? Do you swear to the Devil that it was Lombardi?" Carlow nodded and Devlin turned to Nicholas. "I think he's finally telling the truth."

Nicholas started putting away his knives. "We'll be leaving now, Johnny. You're alive only because I promised the Devil not to kill you tonight. I'll be back tomorrow. You have until then to leave Harbor City. You could, of course, call Lombardi and tell him what happened, but he likes informants less than I do."

Devlin stepped away from Carlow, keeping his gun on him. He walked over to Nicholas. "Ready to go?" he asked. Nicholas made as if to leave, then turned and planted one more knife in the closet door. This one landed just slightly above the last, catching the cotton of Carlow's boxers, but not touching any part of his body. All Carlow saw, however, was the knife landing where he definitely did not want it to be, and fainted. He fell forward with a tearing of fabric. When he hit the floor, his boxers were still hanging from the closet.

"That," Nicholas explained to Devlin, "was for calling me Nicky."

The early morning hours saw a white convertible leaving the city for the mountains in the western part of the state. The top was up, and its driver wore a hat and sunglasses to hide her features from anyone who chanced to look inside.

Angela Martinelli had thought about her father's situation and trusted no one but herself to see him safely back in Harbor City. It was likely that Nicholas and Devlin were right, and that no harm would come to him, but it was also true that someone wanted her father to go to jail. Not that the charges could be sustained in a trial, but it was enough to put him behind bars. There, he would be a target for whoever had set him up.

It was just as likely that this unknown person would prefer that her father never saw the inside of a cell. If she had been arranging things, Angela would ambush her target before he could be brought into the city, and make it look like he had been rescued. The supposed escape of a major crime boss, coupled with the murder of the troopers who had been transporting him, would be enough to cause the State and the Harbor City Police departments to crush that boss's organization, and see the rest of his men either dead or in prison. This would leave the way open for an easy take-over of the vacant territory.

If she could think of this, so could others. Angela drove west.

The area around the barracks where her father was being held was crisscrossed with plenty of side and access roads. There was, however, only one main road that led back into the central part of the state and so to Harbor City. Still, it was not a major highway, but a simple two-lane blacktop through the woods. It was all very scenic, and much favored by Sunday drivers out from the city. There were a number of rest stops and picnic areas just off the road. The troopers would be taking her father along this route.

As Angela drove toward the barracks, she stayed alert for any possible signs of a potential ambush. Keeping to the speed limit, she was passed by several cars going her way, and saw quite a few coming the other way, their drivers on the way to work in the city.

One set of commuters was going to be late. At one of the rest stops was a car on a jack, its driver working on a wheel with a tire iron. His suit coat was being held by another man, who was also holding his own jacket. The white shirt of the man holding the coats was already stained with dirt from the spare that was propped up against a nearby tree. A woman in a not too expensive business suit, probably a secretary of some sort, was looking at her watch. No doubt she had one of those "Late is late, no excuses, you'll work tonight to make up for this" bosses. Angela saw all this and was glad she was not in the 9 to 5 world, much preferring the excitement of her father's life, despite its dangers and drawbacks.

Angela got to the barracks just after seven. She parked in front of a roadside diner which no doubt did a good business on Sundays serving lunch to city motorists out for a drive, but which made much more money feeding hungry state troopers. It was almost shift change, and the diner was full of State Police having breakfast and a last cup of coffee before starting their day.

Angela ordered coffee and eggs, and sat watching out the window. She picked up a discarded paper and looked through it as the place cleared out. Soon, the troopers just off shift would be coming in to unwind after their tour. Then it would be time for her to leave.

As tired State cops came in talking about the problems they had faced and arrests they had made the night before, Angela paid her bill and left. Before getting into her car, she put the convertible's top down and threw her hat and dark glasses into the back seat. She started the car and headed back the way she came. As she drove off, she noted a patrol wagon warming up by the side entrance, her father's ride back to Harbor City.

As she retraced her route, Angela was again alert to any sign of an ambush. She again passed the trio trying to change that tire. They didn't seem to have made any progress. They took no notice of her as she drove by. Angela pulled into the next rest stop. She took what she needed from her purse, left her car, and found a path through the trees that lead back toward the police barracks.

Angela found a position where she could observe the three people. As she suspected, the man with the tire iron was just kneeling on the ground, making no effort to remove the tire. The woman kept her eyes more toward the station than the car. Up close, the man holding the coats was hiding something beneath them.

Eventually, the man on the ground stood up and gestured up the road. In the distance, Angela could see the patrol wagon coming toward them. The trio then took a stand behind the car. The man with the coats dropped them to reveal a machine gun. The other man opened the trunk and came up with a shotgun. The woman produced a pistol of some sorts. All three had their backs to Angela.

They were easy targets. Angela had not spent the last three years just doing her father's books. She had learned much from him and those he trusted. Now she would put at least one of those lessons to practice.

None of the three heard the muffled coughs from Angela's silenced pistol. The woman did not even notice anything wrong until both of her companions had fallen. She turned when the man with the shotgun brushed against her as he went down. Looking for where the shots had come from did her no good. Safely concealed in the woods and well within the range for her pistol, Angela shot the woman down as calmly as she had the two men.

Quickly making sure that none of the three bodies could be seen from the road, Angela walked back through the woods the way she came. She returned to her car and was away before the patrol wagon carrying her father could pass. She stayed ahead of the wagon until it pulled into Prisoner Receiving at the Harbor City Circuit Court Building.

"Any trouble on the trip down?" The guard receiving Martinelli asked the troopers.

"Nah, we thought there might be, what with Martinelli here being some sort of big shot, but it turned out to be a Sunday drive."

The jail guard took Martinelli's arm. "Come on, big shot, we got a nice cell in the executive wing all picked out for you."

As he had since his arrest, Martinelli went willingly. He had not said anything to anyone, except to answer those questions that the law required he should. He had offered no one any resistance, gave no one an excuse to use "justifiable force." He accepted insults with the same calm demeanor as he did kindness. He would remember who had offered which. The kindness would eventually be repaid, as would any other treatment.

Martinelli was placed in the same cell had held Stefano and Prestone. It had been cleaned since their deaths, and there was no trace of what had happened to them. Martinelli, having been cut off from the news since his flight, was not aware of his former employees' fate.

When his eyes had adjusted to the darkness of the cell, Martinelli assessed his situation. He had not given any orders to kill the judge, so any evidence against him had been manufactured. What had been made could be unmade, so all that was left was to survive until matters could be arranged. If bail was not set, he had enough loyal soldiers in the city jail, both guards and prisoners, to protect him. With nothing else to do, Martinelli started to lie down to take a nap. That was when he noticed that he was not alone in his cell.

Before Martinelli could cry out or react, the figure stepped out of the shadows just long enough to be recognized.

"You are an odd choice for a guardian angel, Sergeant Devlin."

The Devil smiled and motioned Martinelli to stay quiet. Then he stepped back into the corner to wait.

He did not have to wait very long. Martinelli had been in his cell about an hour, and had managed a brief nap, when he was woken by the loud closing of the cell block door.

"Be ready," came a whispered warning from the corner.

A uniformed guard approached with a meal tray. "Lunch time, Martinelli."

"I'm not very hungry, thank you. Just leave it and I'll eat it later."

"Whatever you say, I just thought you were entitled to a last meal."

Feigning surprise, Martinelli stood up from the cot. He recognized the guard as one of his own men.

As he had before, the guard pulled the silencer from his pocket and took his time attaching it to the barrel of his pistol. He enjoyed this, watching helpless victims realize that they were going to die, knowing they were trapped.

"Johnny Carlow sends his best." He taunted Martinelli as he tightened the silencer. That was when the Devil stepped out of the shadows.

Firing from the corner, the Devil's first shot struck the gunman in the shoulder. The look of pleasure on the uniformed thug's face quickly changed to one of surprise as Devlin's next shot hit him in the chest. He dropped the gun and fell back against the bars of the cell across the hallway. He had one last look at the Devil getting ready for a third shot before all expression left his face forever.

"Carlow?" Martinelli wanted to ask, but the reports of the two shots in the stone cell were still ringing in his ears. He realized that any questions would have to wait until both men's hearing returned.

Sometime later, in a different cell, Devlin filled Martinelli in on all that had happened.

"So where is Carlow now? You have him locked up somewhere?"

"Well . . ." The Devil took his time answering. He got up and checked that there were no listeners in the hallway. "The official story is that we met on condition that I give him 24 hours to leave the city, and that I brought Nicholas along as a witness to both his statement and my behavior."

"That, at least, is believable. You have been prone to excess lately, but we'll let that pass for now. Just where is my former lieutenant?"

"Nicholas and I made a deal. He agreed not to cut Johnny up into unrecognizable pieces if I agreed to let him go after questioning. That will give us each an equal chance of catching up with him later."

"And if you catch him first?"

"Johnny will turn State's evidence in exchange for a lifetime of protection."

"And if someone else finds him first?"

The Devil looked Louis Martinelli right into the eyes so there would be no misunderstanding. "As long as I don't have any evidence that Johnny Carlow is dead, I'm not going to lose any sleep over him."

Martinelli's hearing was held in the afternoon. Devlin testimony's that Johnny Carlow had admitted to arranging the murder of Judge Calvert at the behest of Jonas Lombardi was enough to free Martinelli. However, the judge, who had at first been reluctant to allow the Devil in his courtroom, refused to issue a warrant for Lombardi based on hearsay from a rival gang member. A warrant was issued for Carlow, however. That warrant stayed open and Johnny Carlow was never again seen in Harbor City, or anywhere else.

It was late in the evening of the following day, almost closing time at Martinelli's. Once again, Frank Devlin made his way to the back door of the restaurant. This time he was expected.

It was just two for dinner. Nicholas served, as usual, but he did not remain in the room after the food was placed on the table. Angela stayed just long enough to thank Devlin for all he had done for her father.

During her brief time at the table, Devlin had noticed something different about the Martinelli girl. ("She's more than a girl," a part of his brain told him.) Nicholas too, had noticed a change in Miss Angela, and wondered if it had anything to do with her unexplained absence.

Louis Martinelli was too worried about the brief but too frequent looks that his angel was exchanging with the Devil to notice any change. He asked her if she minded if he and the sergeant could eat alone, as they had important matters to discuss. Angela did mind, but could not later explain why. Nonetheless, she obeyed her father and left the two men alone.

"You owe me." Devlin stated bluntly after the meal was finished.

"I fail to see how, Sergeant. After all, you started this by your antics in the courtroom. Everything else was just your putting matters right."

Devlin took a deep breath. Men with guns he could master. Reprimands from the Chief and criticism in the newspapers came with the job. This was different. This was a gamble he was taking, and he had to get it right the first time.

"Mr. Martinelli, your involvement in the death of Judge Calvert was ordained once he was revealed to be involved in the death of your aunt. Even without 'my antics,' I believe it possible that you would have at least been questioned and possibly jailed once his honor disappeared."

"That is possible, I'll grant you that, Sergeant. And you did bring her actual killer to your own kind of justice, however quick and relatively painless it was for him. So we are even on that score. How do I owe you?"

"I could have stopped there, let things take their course. Brought to trial, you would have probably been acquitted, but you would have had to survive to the trial. Past events have shown that not to have been likely."

Devlin paused and took a sip of wine, giving Martinelli the chance to comment. The other man stayed silent, and Devlin continued.

"I risked my job for you. If the Commissioner or the press found out about my coming to Nicholas, or about how we questioned Carlow, I'd have a private license and a cheap office right now. Instead, I went ahead and cleared your name, exposed a traitor in your organization, revealed which gang boss tried to frame you, and finally, saved your life."

"And why, Sergeant, why would you take the chance of dealing with the enemy, knowing that your own exposure would mean disgrace or even imprisonment?"

"For this moment here." Devlin spread his arms wide to take in the restaurant. "To be able to sit here and say, 'You owe me,' and know that that your sense of honor would have to agree with me."

Martinelli formally bowed his head. "I acknowledge the debt."

Both men were silent for a time, pondering the implications. One of the four most powerful gang leaders in the city had admitted being in the debt of a man whose mission it was to oppose him.

The older man finally broke the silence. "This debt I owe, is payment due tonight, or will you one day in the future ask something of me?"

"I'm calling it in now. It's time to deal with the Devil."

"Whatever you ask for, if it is within my power to do it, and does not conflict with my responsibilities, is yours, Sergeant."

"You have people in City Hall, the municipal building, other agencies. I want their names."

"Would that include those in your own force?"

"Of course, especially them."

"What about the courts?"

"Whoever's on your payroll there as well." Devlin saw no need to tell Martinelli that, thanks to Michael Shaw, the courts were being taken care of.

"And to what use will you put this information, Sergeant?"

"I think you know. If they take from you, they're taking from the others. We'll watch them, and learn who else is paying them off. Once we've gathered enough evidence, people start going to jail."

"This will cost. What you ask is high."

"For your freedom, for your reputation, for your life - for anyone one of these the price might be high. For all three, you're getting off cheap."

"Then I will remain in your debt. How may I resolve that?"

"I'll leave that to your sense of honor."

"And Lombardi? What of him?"

"The Law can't touch him. You won't risk another gang war by killing him. I'm sure that you'll deal with him in your own way."

"Or you in yours, Sergeant, or you in yours."

A few days later, the events surrounding the death of Steven Calvert had been forgotten by the papers. Their pages were instead filled with the mystery of a triple murder west of the city. The deceased, two men and a woman, were from out of state, and except for some weapons that could not be traced, the State Police had no leads.

The Sentinel used the story to blast the efficiency of the police in general. To the Post, it was not a city crime. They barely mentioned it. The Globe and the Sun, however, both commented that crimes like that rarely occurred in Harbor City anymore, and suggested that the State Police would benefit by having men like Frank Devlin on their force. As the Globe's editor put it, "Safe streets are worth almost any price, even if we do have to deal with the Devil."

Chapter Six
The Devil's Wake

George Fremont Murphy had a dream, to build the finest, most exclusive hotel on the East Coast. It would attract guests and residents from all over, many of whom would move to Harbor City just to live in his building. Others would plan their vacations based on vacancies in the Fremont Tower. The name "Murphy" would be as famous as Hilton, Staler, or Holiday, and this fame would be based on a single hotel, not a chain of them.

Murphy had elaborate plans for his creation. The first five levels would consist of shopping and restaurants. The stores would sell designer originals, museum quality goods, and one-of-a-kind items found nowhere else in the world. Each restaurant would likewise be unique, each featuring a different cuisine, all of them staffed by the finest chefs in the world. Above and below would be nightclubs, with the grandest of all on the roof. He also planned a casino, looking forward to the day when his wealth and influence, along with that of his guests, would force the state to repeal its antiquated laws against games of chance.

Murphy's hotel would have ten floors set aside for guests, each room a suite, the least of them fit for a prince or president. His guests would be smothered in luxury and service, with private servers and domestics available for those who needed more than the personal touch.

Finally, the remaining four floors would consist of private apartments, available on a one, five or ten year lease. Each apartment would take up a quarter of the floor, and be serviced by a bank of private elevators exclusive to the top floors. To insure that each resident was perfectly at home, management would offer a personal architect and designer to construct and arrange the interior of the apartment to the exact taste of its new owner.

Murphy planned carefully. He had purchased the land on which he planned to build years before he knew he would be ready, just to insure that the site would be his. He hired the finest architects to design his dream, and the area's best contractors to make that dream a reality. He obtained exclusive contracts with European designers for the latest in fashions for his shops. He even went so far as to personally scout new entertainers, to befriend and support them, so that when his nightclubs were ready to open, they would open with big name acts who owed him their careers. There would even be a subway spur to bring people in from the center of the city and see them safely home. Yes, over the years, while he was making his fortune and dreaming his dream, Murphy planned very carefully, so that when it was time to build, everything would be perfect. And it almost was.

In his plans, George Fremont Murphy had allowed for every contingency, had prepared for every possibility - except one. Murphy forgot, or rather, overlooked the fact that he would be building his dream in Harbor City.

He had no trouble getting the hotel built. Murphy had done business all around the world, and always budgeted for kickbacks, bribes, and petty and major theft. He spent freely, hired everyone the union bosses "suggested" he hire, and bought far more building materials than he really needed. He made it clear that, as long as he was permitted to build his hotel on time and without too much interference, everyone would profit. With this attitude, the Fremont Tower rose to the sky on schedule.

Murphy's dream was only a few months away from becoming a reality. It was six in the evening. Most of the workers had gone home for the day. Murphy had finished his weekly walk though and was standing just outside the site's main gate, looking up and admiring his creation. He did not hear the car that came speeding around the corner. Nor did he hear the car that came speeding after the first one. He did hear the gunshots. He turned to the sound in time to see several tons of Detroit's finest come racing toward him. The impact knocked him back through the gate and into what he had planned to be the main drive to the entrance. He died at the foot of the dream he had almost completed. His last words, which no one but the night heard, were "So close, so close."

For all his great business sense, George Fremont Murphy died without having made a will. He had never married, and his death produced more relatives than he had known when he was alive. Each had a lawyer and a perfectly good reason why he or she was entitled to all or part of the Murphy estate. There were favorite uncles and favored nieces. There were supposed children, their mothers secretly married to Murphy in places he had never visited. And there were girlfriends, all of whom claimed to have given him the best months of their lives in exchange for a promise of life-long financial security. In the end, only those who had had the good sense to contribute to the re-election fund of the probate judge got any money for their troubles. Some even got enough to pay their legal fees. The remainder of the Murphy fortune went to the state, to be administered by a trustee appointed by the judge.

The appointed trustee got rich, as did the judge, as they slowly and systematically stripped the estate of its worth. They sold its assets for pennies on the dollar, and then took kickbacks from the buyers. The men behind the judge and trustee also profited, receiving their cut of every transaction. Soon, all that was left of the Murphy holdings was a single building, a once proud dream that was allowed to decay.

With no one to pay the bills, construction on the Fremont Tower halted. During the battle for and the selling of the estate, it fell into disrepair. Electrical service was cut off, plumbing fixtures were stolen and sold for scrap. Stairways partly collapsed. Within ten years of Murphy's death, it was a hollow shell. All attempts to sell it failed, and the dream was scheduled to be torn down.

It was here, on the top floor of the Fremont Tower, in what had been intended to be the finest luxury apartment Harbor City had ever seen, that Frank Devlin finally found Anthony Peterson.

Peterson's disappearance just before the gang war had ended

worried Devlin. The gang boss had had a good reason to leave town – someone had tried to kill him. But the war had been over for some time now, and Peterson had yet to return.

No one knew why. Everyone had expected him to return to town once the fighting had stopped. However, months went by, and there was no word or sighting of Tony Peterson. There were, however, rumors. One had Peterson dead and at the bottom of the harbor. Another had him in the trunk of a car parked at the airport. Still another was that he was the Devil's secret prisoner, and that Devlin was using him to obtain information about the mobs' activities. A fourth was that he had reformed, given up the rackets, and was now helping the police in another city fight their own war on crime. All anyone knew for sure was that his gang continued on, run either by trusted lieutenants or by the very men who had betrayed and killed him. No one really cared which, as long as it did not threaten them or interfere with their activities.

Devlin cared. He was sure that Peterson's continued absence was deliberate, if only because it put the gang leader outside the reach of Harbor City justice. Devlin worked his informants, and sent Peterson's description to other departments looking for some sign of the mobster. It was not until he spoke with another agent of the Commissioner's that he learned just what Peterson had been up to.

Michael Shaw was the head of a very private investigation agency located in New York. His company had been brought in to work undercover in Harbor City court system, gathering evidence against corrupt court personnel. During a meeting with the Commissioner, Shaw warned Devlin that Peterson had been seen in New York, recruiting men who were not afraid of "a small town cop with a fancy nickname."

"Let then come," Devlin had retorted, "They'll find out that every small town has a Boot Hill."

A few weeks following Shaw's warning, Devlin heard from his own informants that Peterson was back in town. No one had seen him, but he was said to have brought new blood into his gang.

Finally, Devlin was tipped to someone who might be able to lead him to Peterson.

"What'll you have, buddy?" The bartender asked absently. There were too many customers in his place for him to give more than half his attention to any one of them.

The newcomer did not bother looking out from under the hat that covered his features. "Beer," he said, in almost a whisper, then muttered something the bartender didn't catch.

"What was that, buddy? Take the soap out of your mouth and try again."

This time the customer did look up, letting the barkeep get a good look at him. "A beer please, Louie," Devlin said clearly, but still in a lowered voice, "With an information chaser."

"Ah Hell, why me? Why tonight you have to come in here? The first good night I have in a week and now you're coming in to shoot somebody. Give me a break, Dev …" Louie almost said the name, then stopped. If anyone heard him, and word got that out that the Devil was in the house, most of his patrons would assume that he was after them. Within minutes, the Devil would be his only customer.

"No killing tonight, Louie, unless you insist. I just need a word or two. We'll have a chat, and I'll leave quietly. Otherwise," Devlin took a quick look around. "Otherwise, I see one or two people that could use arresting, and there will probably be some more in here tomorrow night, and the next, and the …"

"Okay, I get your point. What do you want to know?"

"Word is, you know where Tony Peterson is holed up."

"Could be." This time Louie took a quick look around, to make sure that no one was listening to their conversation. "People talk all the time in here, and don't watch what they say. They forget a bartender has ears."

"And what did these 'people' have to say about Peterson?"

Louie didn't answer right away, as if weighing the consequences of not telling Devlin what he wanted to know against what would happen to him if it came out that he put the finger on Tony

Peterson. Finally, he gave Devlin his answer.

"What the hell! You find Peterson there's no way he's gonna be able to get back at me for telling you about him, not unless his corpse learns to walk."

Louie took another quick look around, then motioned Devlin in closer.

"I heard two of Peterson's men talking the other night. Their boss is hiding out in one of the penthouses in the old Fremont Hotel."

"That's a long walk up from the street."

"I guess that's why he picked it. Who would think of looking for him there?"

"Makes sense. Thanks, Louie, I owe you one."

"Just don't come back any time soon, Devlin, and we'll call it even."

The Devil smiled and nodded his agreement, dropped a bill on the bar next to his untouched beer and left. As he turned to go, he failed to see the sly grin that spread over the bartender's face. After the door had closed behind Devlin, a man came up and had a brief talk with Louie. He left the bar wearing his own self-satisfied smile.

It was late when Devlin got home. He had considered going straight to the Fremont Tower and confronting Peterson that night. But there was no power in the abandoned building, and the darkness would work against him. He did not like the idea of a nineteen-story climb up crumbling stairs, especially in the dark with only a pocket flash to light his way, a flash that would make him a perfect target should his presence be detected. No, he'd wait until early morning, after a good night's sleep. He'd be rested, but Peterson and any men he had with him would no doubt be just getting in. They'd be tired after their night's exertions, looking forward to their beds, and easier prey for the Devil if it came to a fight.

Devlin did not think it would come to that. His carefully built mystique of the Devil was such that most gunmen would not chance a shootout with him. Those that had, had died, and that lesson was not lost on those remaining. Devlin expected to walk into Peterson's hideaway, put the fear of the Devil in him, and leave. He'd reinforce the message that there was nowhere in Harbor City you could hide that the Devil could not find you, and maybe he'd scare Peterson out of town for good.

The next morning, Devlin called the Commissioner's office and left word of his plans. Harbor City's top cop was at the state capital that day, discussing his war against the gangs with the governor.

And the war is going well, Devlin thought. Thanks to Michael Shaw's inside men, corruption in the District Attorney's office and the courts had been cleaned up. Of course, Devlin being responsible for the death of a crooked judge had helped scare a few people into line. The deal Devlin had made with Louis Martinelli had also helped. Martinelli had given Devlin the names of the gang contacts in City Hall. "Most of them, anyway," Devlin reminded himself, sure that Martinelli had held back his own best sources.

The efforts of Shaw, Devlin, and the Commissioner had been enough to break the gangs' stranglehold on the city's municipal and judicial systems. Fewer cases were being dropped. Judges suddenly were ruling more in favor of the prosecution than the defense. More and more criminals who had counted on their mob connections to set them free or obtain a reduced sentence found themselves serving long prison terms.

Thinking of Shaw reminded Devlin of the man's warning that Peterson had gone out of town to recruit new talent. Devlin hadn't seen or heard of anyone new in Harbor City, and police informants at Peterson's nightclub had not reported any change in employees or any "new talent" hanging around.

"He probably just wanted some new bodyguards," Devlin decided as he started the long climb up to the Fremont Tower penthouses.

It took Devlin over thirty minutes to climb to the Penthouse level. He rested every fourth flight, not wanting to be out of breath when he reached the top. Twice he had to walk to the other end of the floor he was on, the stairs having collapsed between the fourth and fifth floors, and held on by only a few rusted bolts between the ninth and tenth. With no power to the building, the hallways were lit only by the sunlight coming in through large picture windows. At least he didn't have to use his flash and give his position away to any watchers that might be present. Finally, he reached the seventeenth floor.

From the stairwell door, Devlin could see the doors to each of the four luxury apartments. They were all standing open. There was no one standing watch, and, listening carefully, he could hear no sounds coming out of any of the rooms. Revolver drawn and at the ready, he moved quietly down the hallway and entered the first suite. No Peterson. Nor was he in any of the other three rooms on that floor.

Devlin checked the eighteenth and nineteenth floors with the same result. No Peterson and no sign that he or anyone else had used any of the rooms in quite a few years. Convinced that he had been given a bum steer, Devlin decided to give the twentieth floor the same careful search and then go home, rest up, and that evening close up Louie's bar, doing as much damage as possible as a warning against lying to the Devil.

Devlin made the same careful approach to the twentieth floor. He neither saw nor heard anyone as he got to the top of the stairway and checked the hall. Again the first suite he checked was empty, but his discovery in Apartment 2002 changed his plans for the evening.

When he first entered the Fremont Tower, Devlin had not been quite sure as to what to expect. He might have been on a fool's errand, sent there by a bartender with a soon to be broken funny bone. He might have found Tony Peterson asleep, or plotting his Harbor City comeback with a new band of picked men, or just hiding out from both the Law and his former associates. What he did not expect was to find Tony Peterson, once one of Harbor

City's top underworld bosses, lying dead on the floor with a note pinned to his chest.

Peterson was sprawled on the floor of what would have been the living room. He had been shot several times.

He was sure that Peterson was dead, but out of habit and training Devlin checked anyway. From the condition of the body it seemed that Peterson had been killed sometime yesterday. Devlin leaned over the body to read the note pinned to the chest.

"The long night of the Devil is done. Now is the hour of the Wolf."

A trap! Twenty stories up in a building no doubt filling with men right now.

"Well, Tony," Devlin addressed the corpse. "I don't suppose this was the way either of us expected to meet again. Who is this Wolf, and how did he manage to turn things around on you?"

As he talked to the ghost of Peterson, Devlin searched the body looking for anything he might use in his coming fight.

"Whoever this Wolf character is, Tony, he lead me right into it. It was no secret that I was looking for you, so he had me tipped to the bartender. Louie was probably in on it too. Well, I'll deal with him if, no, when I get out of here." Peterson was clean. Devlin didn't find anything on his body that could help him.

"Louie probably tipped Wolf off just after I left his place. That would fit in with your time of death. Wolf probably brought you up here the same day I got the tip-off. Nice, gets rid of you and me in the same trap. At least he had the decency to warn me by leaving this hokey note."

Devlin considered his situation. Wolf no doubt had someone watching the building, with men not too far off. The watcher would have notified Wolf as soon as Devlin entered. Give fifteen minutes for the gunmen to gather, another thirty for them to disperse throughout the tower, blocking the stairs and exits.

"They're all in position now," Devlin realized. He cursed himself for falling into the trap, and then for not bringing back-up. "At least I let the Chief know where to look for my body," he said bitterly.

He checked his weapons. He had a .38 revolver with two full reloads. He left that hooked on his belt for now. He took his .45 derringer out of its sleeve holster and dropped it into his pocket. The .32 he usually kept strapped to his left ankle he now held in his right hand. That made twenty-five rounds. His two throwing knives made twenty-seven.

"I just hope your friend didn't send twenty-eight men."

With a final nod to the corpse of Tony Peterson, the Devil stepped out into Hell.

Devlin took only a few steps into the hallway when he ducked back into Apartment 2002. He did so in time to avoid the gunfire that had come from either end of the hall. He quickly picked up Peterson's body and, standing it upright, pushed it out of the door. As soon as he released it, he fired one shot at an angle down the hall. There were answering shots, and the body jerked as it was hit from both sides.

The two gunmen were surprised that it had ended this quickly. They had expected a better fight from this cop called the Devil. They were even more surprised a few seconds later.

Crouching low, Devlin turned first to the man nearest him. One of his throwing knives took the man in the throat. The second man, his attention more on the corpse in front of him than on his partner, failed to see the Devil pivot and stand with his gun in his left hand. Devlin's bullet took him in the chest.

Devlin relieved both men of their pistols. Automatics were not the Devil's weapons of choice, but he was in no position to be picky. He dropped his .32 into his pocket and, .45 in each hand, ran to the stairwell.

Standing on the landing, Devlin looked over the rail and saw three more men climbing his way. He rained shots down on them. Two dropped as the large caliber bullets pierced their skulls. The third had been struck in the arm, and backed off, returning fire. Knowing that to retreat would only give more men time to get into position, the Devil leaped down the flight of steps. The wounded gunman looked up to see the Devil flying toward him. He fired too quickly, and his shots went wild. Devlin returned fire as soon as he landed, emptying the remainder of a clip into the man, spattering the wall behind him with blood.

The Devil dropped the now useless .45s and again took out his revolver. He could hear distant sounds of running feet racing up stairs. Devlin judged them to be several floors below him. He chanced descending two more flights.

Whatever floor they were on, the sound of gunfire would have brought anyone on the other side of the building down the halls toward him. As the Devil reached the seventeenth floor, he glanced quickly down the corridor. No one there. He left the stairway and moved quietly toward the rooms. He made it halfway down the hall when he saw the door at the other end opening.

Hoping he had not been seen, the Devil took refuge in the room nearest him. This room was smaller than the rest, and Devlin recognized it as the servant's area. From here they would receive meals sent up from the sub-basement kitchens and deliver them to the guests. It was here that he waited. He knew what he had to do next. Six months ago, he would not have even contemplated it. He had believed in fair play, in the lessons of the law and the rights of all men, accused of crime or not. That was before he had become the Devil, given the mission to end the gang rule of Harbor City by any means necessary. Even then, anyone he had faced had always been given a better than even chance to take him down before they faced the Devil's justice. Today, trapped and hunted, those rules no longer applied.

The man some called demon and still others savior waited behind a mostly closed door as one, two, then a third man went by, all walking in a line, all of them watching the stairs in front of them. They were waiting for the Devil to appear, not knowing he was already among them. As the last man passed his room, the Devil reached out.

Wrapping his right arm around the third man's throat, Devlin stabbed upward with his remaining knife. Then, heaving the corpse aside, the Devil stepped into the hall, reversed his knife and sent it flying into the back of the second man. The thud of that body falling was drowned out by the roar of the Devil's revolver, the third man falling before he could turn. He turned his back on his three would-be killers and made it down the hall to the opposite side stairs.

Stopping to listen, he heard no noises in the stairwell either above or below him. They would all be on the other side, though some would now be trying to find the floor where his last shot had been fired. It would not take them long, and then they'd be coming down these stairs. His .32 now in his left hand and his .38 in his right, the Devil ran down the stairs, his feet just barely lighting on the metal tread caps.

He could not keep this up. Sooner or later he would lose the guessing game he was playing with his pursuers and find himself trapped between floors. He was also sure that Wolf had left men at the bottom of each stairway just in case he made it that far. The Devil had to change the odds in his favor. So when he reached the tenth floor, he stopped and waited.

He waited until he heard footsteps above him, then he fired a single shot to let them know where he was. He then ran through the tenth floor doorway.

The Devil was betting his life that some of those on the stairs would suspect an ambush and that only one or two would follow him down the hall. He was right. As fast as he had run into the hall, he stopped and turned, in time to gun down the three men who had carelessly rushed the door.

He could have reached the other side without incident, which made him wonder about how well this Wolf had organized his men. Had the Devil planned this hunt, it would have been more systematic, with each floor secured before the next was searched. But that was not the gangster mentality. Even in groups, they acted for themselves and on impulse.

Wolf, whoever he is, probably offered a bonus to the one who brought me down, thought the Devil, *and everybody's trying to cash in. Well, thank heaven for small favors.*

With everyone now heading back to the other side, or so he hoped, the Devil stepped over the bodies of his last three kills and took the stairs to the 9th floor. Only then did he go down the hall to the opposite end of the building.

"There can't be too many of them left," Devlin said to himself. "And with luck, they're all on this side."

The Devil approached the ninth floor stairwell cautiously. If he was right, his remaining foes should now be grouped just above him, figuring him to keep to his previous pattern and emerge from the tenth floor doorway. He hoped they had been too interested in killing him to have noticed what he had seen on his way up.

The door was partially open. That was good. It allowed Devlin to look up without being seen. There was one man on the steps above him. He could see the shadows of two more who were standing on the landing between the tenth and eleventh floors. The Devil gave a grateful look at the rusty bolts that were the reason he had avoided these particular steps on the way up. He hoped that the work crews who had installed them had cut the usual Harbor City corners.

Devlin emptied his .32 toward the men in the stairwell. He saw one go down, which was good, but not his sole purpose. He wanted to draw out any more that were still in the hallways. If there were no more, fine, he could handle the remaining two. If there were more, several more, even better.

Three more men joined the ones on the landing. The Devil fired another shot to keep them interested, and to draw their fire to cover up the creaking noises coming from the stairs. Devlin eyed the rusted bolts appreciatively, then quickly stood in the doorway and dry-fired his .32. At the click, the Devil very noticeably retreated. The five men followed, convinced that the Devil was out of ammo and on the run.

The combined weight of all five gangsters was too much for the weakened bolts. They gave way, and the stairs and men followed. The collapse took out the remainder of the stairs on this side of the building. The Devil doubted if any of the gunmen had survived the fall.

With no other choice, The Devil walked down the hall again. He was tired, but it was almost over. Any thugs left would be waiting at the bottom of the stairs. Devlin looked over his shoulder toward the collapsed stairway. Well, maybe not on that side, he thought.

Devlin stopped at the door to the stairs and listened. He heard nothing but his own heartbeat. He holstered his .32 and took time to reload his .38. He took out the derringer from its place in his sleeve and, with a gun in each hand, he carefully descended the steps. His progress halted at the fifth floor.

The stairs on this side were out. Devlin had noted this in his climb up, but had forgotten it until just now. He thought about jumping down a floor, but the angle was wrong. He'd either miss his landing and fall a flight or two, or the weight of his body would be enough to loosen the bolts on this side.

"So now what do I do?" the Devil asked himself as he tried to figure a way down.

Forty-five minutes after his men had entered the Fremont Tower, Wolf Hopkins checked his watch for the third time, then resumed watching the building through his binoculars.

"They've been in there long enough. Someone should have signaled."

The man with him shrugged his shoulders. "Maybe this Devlin is as tough as Peterson said he was."

"It doesn't matter. I told them thirty minutes, and it's now past that. No one's come out, so Devlin's still in there. Blow it."

The man with Hopkins put aside his own binoculars and bent down to the black box that was at his feet. He pulled up slowly on the plunger that was sticking out of its top, then quickly pushed it back down. In an instant, shaped charges with which Hopkins had previously mined the first floor of the Fremont Tower went off. The explosions blew out the supports of the building and brought it crashing down.

"If Devlin was still alive, that should finish him. The Devil's dead, my friend. Let's get settled in our new town."

It was some months ago, during the gang wars, when he read of his own death in the Harbor City papers, that Anthony Peterson decided he should take a brief vacation. There had been a correction in the following editions but by then Peterson was packed and on a train out of town. He stayed for some time in Florida, enjoying the sun, sand, and girls. He occasionally called a trusted lieutenant to make sure his businesses, honest and otherwise, were all running smoothly. When he heard that peace had been made between the gangs, he thought about returning, but things were going so well back home without him that he felt that he could stay away without trouble.

Thinking of trouble caused Peterson to think of the Devil. The mobs in Harbor City had had smooth sailing until he appeared on the scene. City Hall, the courts, the D.A.'s office had all been fixed. The police were all mostly straight arrows, but that would change as soon as the mayor convinced the governor to let him appoint the next commissioner. That done, someone could take care of the current one, and Harbor City would once again be an open town, just like the good old days. Even Capone had once wished he had set up in Harbor City rather than in Chicago.

But the "good old days" were gone, and not likely to come back, thanks to the Devil. He had broken two gangs, and would likely continue to cause trouble for the rest until he or they were gone. Peterson had no desire to live in an honest town, so the Devil had to go.

Easy to say, harder to do, Peterson thought. Many of Harbor City's best gunmen had tried to take down the lawman and had failed. Peterson finally decided to look elsewhere, and that decision had led him to New York City.

New York had always had more than its share of gangs. Even during the thirties and forties, when the mobs had been plagued by all sorts of self-appointed crime fighters, the gangs continued to flourish. Today those private crime fighters were gone, retired, or buried, but the gangs they fought against were still operating.

Peterson made a few calls, and was soon on another train back north, taking care to detour around Harbor City.

His contacts in New York were not much help to him at first. The gunmen to whom Peterson was first introduced were no better than the ones he had left in Harbor City, the ones the Devil had no trouble gunning down. His search soon brought him to the waterfront, and to the Red Thorn. He had been told to ask for Wolf Hopkins.

The Red Thorn had the same reputation as did the legendary Pink Rat and Black Ship, bars where the police did not dare go, except in force, and then only when absolutely necessary. No undercover cops would work these places, for fear of what would happen to them should they be discovered.

As Peterson walked into the bar, the background hum of conversation suddenly stopped. He felt every eye on him. In the silence, he thought he heard the slides of one or two automatics pulled back. Without making any sudden moves, Peterson slowly walked over to the counter. The bartender came and stood in front of him.

"Beer," he said. The barkeep did not move. He did not serve just anyone at the Red Thorn.

Peterson knew that he was the stranger, but as a gang boss, he was not used to being ignored, much less challenged. He tried again.

"Beer, please." The bartender still did nothing but stare at him.

"Beer, or a mop." That got a response.

"What do you want a mop for?"

"Because if you don't bring me a beer, I'm going to shoot you in your damn head, and I like to clean up after myself."

The bartender looked past Peterson, and after receiving a signal of some sort, pulled him a beer from the tap.

Peterson took a long sip, then asked, "Hopkins here?"

As if expecting the question, the bartender pointed in the direction he had just looked. "Over there, last booth."

Peterson picked up his beer and walked over to the booth against the far wall. The man in the booth had already taken the seat that allowed him to keep his back to everyone else in the place. Peterson sat opposite him without waiting to be invited.

"You're Hopkins?"

The man in the booth did not bother answering the obvious question. "And you are Anthony Peterson, recently from Florida, less recently from Harbor City. I'm told you are looking for some talent to take back home with you."

"What else were you told?"

As Peterson waited for an answer, he studied the man across the table. Hopkins was large, well-groomed and clean shaven, handsome but not pretty. He was not at all what Peterson had expected.

"If you are disappointed in my appearance, you should know that 'Wolf" is my given name, not a silly affectation like some of our kind adopt."

"We don't go much for nicknames in Harbor City, either."

"Except for one man, you don't. At least, that is what I've been given to understand."

"You're talking about the Devil." Hopkins had learned quite a bit about Peterson in the brief time the Harbor City gang boss had been in New York. Peterson, however, knew little beyond the man's name and the reputation he had with those who had directed him to Hopkins.

The New Yorker gave Peterson a brief smile, one that conveyed a certain disappointment in his out of town guest.

"I'm talking about a cop named Frank Devlin, a man whom you and your fellows have glorified into a crime fighting myth with that stupid name you've given him. Make a man a legend, you make people afraid of him, then he's harder to kill."

Peterson was already impressed with Hopkins. The man had a certain style, reminding him of Louis Martinelli back home. He was plain speaking, and was familiar with at least part of the problem. He felt that he was talking to an equal, not just some gunman he was hiring for a job. Of course, had they been back in Harbor City, it would have been Peterson giving the audience.

"And what do you think of Frank Devlin, Hopkins?"

Hopkins bent forward and looked Peterson direct in the eyes. "He's a man, not a devil. A man can be hunted, he can be trapped, and he can be killed. If that is what you need done, I can do it."

"Then you'll provide me with someone from your organization to do the job?"

"Pay attention, Peterson. I said that *I* will do it. I don't have an organization, like you down there, or some of the ones here. I have a few boys who work with me. I have others who work for me when I need a larger gang. I make my money the old fashion way. I steal it, I hurt people for it, I kill people for it. There have been those who have paid me not to hurt or kill them. I don't go in for a big gang, because that attracts attention."

"But what kind of support do you have if one of your men gets caught?"

"My men don't usually get caught. If they do, they do their time quietly and they stay on the payroll. If they should talk, they know that I'll kill whomever they love."

"What if a man doesn't love anybody?"

"Everybody loves someone, if only himself."

"When can you start?"

"I've already started. Tonight I'll have one of my men head down to Harbor City to look things over. You'll stay with me and tell me all about your hometown. We'll talk about this devil that has everyone down there wetting their pants. In a week, we'll leave. In two weeks your devil will be dead."

Two weeks later found Hopkins and Peterson on the top floor of the Fremont Tower.

"Yes, this building will be perfect. You've done as I've asked, Tony?"

"Yes, I've had the word put out that I'm back in town. Tonight, Devlin will get the tip about Louie. That should lead him here." Peterson wandered over to the window and looked out over Harbor City.

"That's good, Tony. As soon as he enters, my spotter will notify me. I'll then have my men and yours come in after him. They'll be nearby, it should not take more than a quarter hour for them to gather. They'll then have thirty minutes to bring him down."

Peterson turned away from his view and back toward Hopkins. "And if they don't."

"Oh, they should. One man, trapped twenty stories in the air, fighting alone against a gang, what chance does he have? None really, the way I've planned it."

"What makes you think he'll come alone?"

"He will, Peterson, he will. He's bought into his own legend."

"You know, Wolf, I still don't understand why we don't just take him down when he enters the building, or as he climbs the stairs."

"As soon as the trap is sprung, he will begin his escape. If he is as good as you say he is, then the higher he is, the harder for him to escape."

"The back-up plan, why not just go with that?"

"We could, but I would rather it be known for certain that Devlin's dead. I would really like to have a body for the wake."

Hopkins walked passed Peterson to the window the gang boss had just abandoned. "My only regret, Tony, is that Devlin won't know the name of the man who killed him."

"Is that important?"

"Not really. Still, it would be nice."

"I thought you tough New Yorkers didn't go in for that sort of thing."

"Well, Tony, I'm not in New York right now, am I?" Hopkins turned and reached into his pocket and brought out a notebook and pen. He briefly wrote something and tore out the page.

"That should do it, don't you think?"

"A bit melodramatic, isn't it, Wolf?"

"I admit it's not very good, but the best I can do under the circumstances."

"How can you be sure that Devlin will see it?"

Without answering, Hopkins again turned and looked out the window.

"Tony, I've been thinking. This isn't really such a bad town. Smaller than back home, but in some ways just the same. Someone like me could do well here."

"Things aren't the same here, Wolf. For one thing, the bosses would not let you operate the way you do back home."

"But none of them knows I'm here."

"I know."

Hopkins turned to face Peterson, drawing his gun.

"Yes, and you're the only one, aren't you?"

Soon after, Hopkins left alone, leaving Peterson as bait for his trap.

Within twenty-four hours after the building came down, the rumor spread across the city. Within forty-eight hours the spotters who had watched Devlin go into the Fremont Tower but had not seen him come out before its collapse confirmed it - the Devil was dead! Within seventy-two hours, the party was planned.

The celebration was to be held where the Devil was born - in Dave's Place. Dave's Place was in Northeast Harbor City, just off Blair Rd. It was a common meeting ground for all the gangs. It was there that Sergeant Frank Devlin had killed his first two men, and acquired the name "the Devil." Whoever planned the party must have felt that this was an appropriate setting for Devlin's wake.

The evening the party was to be held, Harbor City's Police Commissioner held a special meeting in his office. Present, beside himself, were Detective Sergeant Benjamin Campbell, Anton Szold, and the private operative Michael Shaw.

"Are we sure he's dead?" the Commissioner asked.

"It's been four days, boss. If he were alive, we'd have heard from him by now."

"Unless, Sergeant," rebutted Szold, "He is still trapped beneath the rubble of the Fremont Tower."

"I hope not, Sir." Seeing the shock on everyone's face, Campbell went on to explain.

"When that building blew, the penthouse wound up on the street. The rest of it collapsed down into the sub-basements. Even with crews working twenty-four hours a day, it'll be another week before they clear it all away. If Devlin's trapped down there, he's facing a long slow death. I'd rather he went when it first came down."

From his place in the corner, Michael Shaw spoke up. "The question now, is what do we do to avenge this man. He died a hero's death. He needs a fitting memorial."

Without a word, the Commissioner looked toward Campbell.

"We've shut this city down. Peterson's place is locked up tight. I've had the Health Department shut down Martinelli's restaurant on a few flimsy technicalities. For the first time in I don't know how long, Lombardi's floating casino has been dry docked. As far as the gangs are concerned, Harbor City is closed."

Campbell turned toward Szold. "Sir, I'm afraid that you'll be getting more than your usual number of complaints about how the men have been treating certain of our less upstanding citizens. Without sweeping anything aside, I do ask you to be a little understanding."

Campbell got a nod from the IAD chief and hoped that served as a positive reply.

"How about this 'Wolf' character? Any word on him, Sergeant?" Campbell shook his head. "How about your sources, Michael?"

"I've called New York. No ones heard anything about Hopkins

returning there. If he does, he'll be dealt with." Shaw waited for someone to voice an objection to this obvious death sentence. When no one did, he continued.

"Hopkins has probably gone to ground somewhere in Harbor City. It will be awhile before we hear from him again. In the meantime," Shaw paused until everyone was looking his way. "I suggest we get ready for a party."

Shaw took a brace of .45 semi-automatic pistols from the briefcase on the floor by his feet. The Commissioner reached into the bottom drawer of his desk and brought out two more.

"My thinking exactly, Michael." The police chief looked at Campbell. "Sergeant, any plans for tonight?"

"I was going to stay home and watch TV, but I can change my plans, if you have a couple more of those cannons."

"Here, Sergeant." Shaw produced two more pistols from his bag, leaving Campbell to wonder just what else was in there.

"Commissioner. There is no basis for a police raid on this bar. I really can't go along with this."

"No one's asking you too, Anton. First of all, this is not a 'police raid.' Is that understood by everyone?" Shaw and Campbell both nodded. "The three of us are going to a public place to have a few drinks off duty. If trouble breaks out, we will deal with it as best we can." He looked over toward Shaw. "Do you think trouble will break out, Michael?"

"I'm sure of it."

"Secondly, Anton, it's possible that I may not come back from tonight's outing. If so, then there's a letter in my desk appointing you Acting Commissioner should anything happen to me."

The Commissioner stood up, and looked at the guns on his desk. "I once offered these to Devlin. He turned them down. He said that a good cop didn't need that kind of firepower, that he always had a trick or two up his sleeve. Well, it looks like he finally ran out of tricks."

The Commissioner took off his suit coat, put on a shoulder harness with holsters for both guns, then slipped his coat back on.

"Gentlemen, if you are ready, let's paint the town red."

At the same time that the Commissioner was having his meeting, Louis Martinelli walked through his empty restaurant looking for his daughter Angela. She was not in the kitchen, nor in the office. He tried her room. Finally, he went down to the basement workroom.

Angela was bent over the workbench, quietly cleaning a gun. There was another weapon placed to the side, awaiting her attention.

"Angel."

"Yes, Father?"

"May I ask what you are doing?"

"I'm getting ready for a party."

"No."

With that word, Angela turned on her father. Before she could speak, Martinelli held up his hand to silence her. Only her love for the man, and many years of obeying him, kept her silent.

"Angela, my dear, my darling child, I know that when I was suspected of having that judge killed, while I was in jail for that, you and Sergeant Devlin became close. I also know that since then, you and he have been seeing each other." Martinelli smiled at the surprised look on her face.

"Ah, you thought that your poor old papa did not know. Sergeant Devlin probably told you that the Commissioner did not know either. No matter, now." Again, he held up his hand to prevent her interrupting.

"Angela, have I ever lied to you before in the things that matter? No. Well, I promise you that your sergeant will be avenged. He has never done me any harm, and I can do this one thing for him. This Wolf will be hunted down."

"And the party? What about those who are celebrating his death?"

"They will not celebrate long, this I also promise."

The party was in full swing when the Commissioner and Campbell walked through the front door. No one took any notice of them, they were just two more revelers there to celebrate the death of the Devil.

"Where's Shaw?" whispered Campbell.

"He's here, somewhere. Michael has always been one to blend in with the crowd and then show up when needed. And Ben, with the noise in here, I don't think you have to whisper."

"No, Sir."

"And watch the title. No sense in pushing our luck. We'll need it later."

The pair found a place in the back, against a wall. Unasked, a waiter put a pitcher of beer on the table.

"Beer's free, tonight, anything else, pay at the bar."

"Who do we thank for that?" Campbell asked, hoping he had never arrested the man.

"The bosses, they're throwing this wingding. Lombardi's over there," he gestured toward a front corner with his tray, "and Pratt's over at the bar."

"What about Peterson and Martinelli?"

The waiter looked at the Commissioner as if recognizing him. He did not, however, place his face with the one he has seen so often in the paper.

"Word is that Peterson ain't coming back. Martinelli, he may have helped put this together, but he's got too much class for a joint like this."

After the waiter left, the two men sat sipping their beers. Campbell tried to pick Shaw out of the crowd.

"When do we move, boss?"

"Give them some more drinking time, and go easy on yours. Another thirty minutes should do it."

"Gentlemen, a toast!"

The man at the bar had to shout several times before the room quieted down enough for him to be heard, but since he was Harry Pratt, gang boss and one of the hosts of the party, everybody soon stopped talking to hear what he had to say.

"A toast, Gentlemen! To the Devil!"

"The Devil!" shouted some of the crowd. The rest waited for the rest of the toast.

"He was a pain in the butts of all of us here. To the Devil! May he rot in hell!"

A ragged chorus answered back as all but three men drained their glasses. Campbell could see that the Commissioner was almost ready to start things off, but then another voice was heard.

"Another toast!" Again the speaker had to wait until the crowd was silent. Then Jonas Lombardi spoke.

"To the man who did what we could not. If the Wolf is here, let him come and claim credit. If not, let's drink to him now, and we'll reward him later."

"To the Wolf!"

There were shouts of 'Wolf, Wolf' until it became clear that the villain of the hour was not in the room.

"Sounds like a kennel, doesn't it, boss?" But Campbell got no reply. He looked over toward his chief and saw that he was ready for action. Then he looked over toward the door.

"Wait a minute, boss, something's happening."

The front door to Dave's Place slowly opened, and a man stood waiting to be recognized. The first few to see him fell silent, then quickly backed away. Then the whispers started, and before long, all eyes were to the front.

"Sweet suffering martyrs!" exclaimed Campbell.

The Devil stood there in the doorway, arms down by his side. Finally, he spoke.

"Okay, who's ready to pay for his sins?"

One gangster in the front of the crowd, nearest the Devil, finally found the courage to say what everyone was thinking.

"But - you're dead."

The Devil looked past the mobster who spoke, and his eyes seemingly met those of each man in the room. He saw Campbell and the Commissioner against the far wall, ready to back whatever move he made. There was a flicker of recognition in his eyes when he spotted Shaw, and the Commissioner's agent nodded his readiness.

"You can't kill the Devil. I'm back from Hell, and before I return, I'm sending each of you fatherless dogs there ahead of me."

Each man knew that tonight, there would be no mercy, no surrender. The Devil had been hunted, killed, and now his death was being celebrated. Those who dared to look into his eyes saw nothing human there. In the eyes of the Devil, they were all guilty.

Campbell did not stop to wonder how Devlin had escaped from the building. All he knew was that the Devil was back. He readied his gun, and saw the Commissioner doing the same. They both realized that with the crowd he was facing, Devlin would need more help than his .38 could provide, and he would not have the time to reload. The mob knew this too, and would try for the second time in a week to bring down the Devil.

The first man to draw died with a knife in his throat, as did the second. As other guns were being drawn, Devlin raised his right arm and brought up the Tommy gun he had been concealing behind his leg. Before anyone else could react, the Devil pulled back the bolt and opened fire.

The men in front died instantly, some cut in two by the spray of the weapon. Others were brought down by Shaw's .45s, the private agent having moved closer to the Devil just before the slaughter began. Hearing the sounds of automatic weapons, the gangsters in the back tried to escape through the rear door. Stopped by Campbell and the Commissioner, they were forced to join the fight.

Panic did much of the Devil's work. Men fell and were trampled. Some used the confusion to settle old scores or to eliminate rivals, only to fall themselves a few minutes later. Others fired blindly, hoping for a lucky shot. Most of these were lucky only for the Devil, as stray shots took down many of his foes.

One such stray bullet killed Jonas Lombardi as he cowered in a corner. Harry Pratt took refuge behind the bar, and thought himself safe, but the cheap plywood was no protection against the bullets that came from the Devil's machine gun.

Finally, it was over. The floor of Dave's Place, where not covered by fallen gunmen, was red with blood. The walls were similarly spattered. Only three men still stood.

Both the Commissioner and Campbell had been hit, Campbell in the arm, the chief in the leg. He had spent the last few minutes propped up against a wall. Neither man's wound was serious enough to be life threatening. Shaw, too, had been wounded. He was bleeding from the shoulder, and his right arm hung limp at his side. His left hand, though, still held a .45 at the ready, as he looked for signs of fight in any of the few wounded survivors. Of the Devil there was no sign.

IV

Sometime later, in a room known only to them, two lovers met. Afterwards, they lay talking.

"So, are you going to tell me how you escaped the explosion?"

Frank Devlin turned to face Angela Martinelli. "I never had to escape the explosion." He told her about the collapsed stairs, and his having no way down.

"Even if there had been stairs, Wolf's gunmen would have been waiting for me. I knew my luck couldn't last forever."

"You were wrong there. It does seem to have lasted a bit longer."

He gave her a hug, then continued. "The Fremont Tower had dumb waiters to bring food up from the sub-basement kitchen. I remembered seeing one in the servants' room on the seventeenth floor. I went to the one in the fifth floor serving area, pulled it up to my level, squeezed in, and lowered myself down. From the kitchens, I made my way to the old subway line. I was half a mile away when Wolf blew the building."

"So why didn't you call me to tell me you were okay?" Devlin could see that, beneath her relief that he was alive, Angela was hurt and angry that she had not been the first one he had called.

"Angela, if you had known I was alive, you would have insisted on coming with me to crash my wake."

"Try another excuse, Dev, the party wasn't planned until after you'd been 'dead' for a day or two."

"The party was planned an hour after I finally got out of that subway and called your father."

"He knew you were alive, and he didn't tell me!"

At least, Devlin thought, *now she's mad at both of us.*

"For the same reason, darling. We didn't want you at the party. None of your father's people were there."

"So you planned it, you and him."

"Right, get all, or rather, most of my enemies in one place, and let things happen as they did. Harbor City will be a more peaceful town now. Pratt and Lombardi are dead, so is Peterson by the way, as are most of the gunmen who worked for them. The gang bosses are gone, and there's no one left with which to form a new one."

Angela sat up. Seeing Devlin's smile, she wrapped a sheet around her. "And why would my father go along with this?"

"Because of what I offered him."

"Which was?"

"Harbor City."

Seeing the confused look on her face, he explained. "I pointed out to your father that, with Peterson, Lombardi, and Pratt out of the way, the city, or at least, the less legal part of it would be his for the taking. Within a week, he'll have taken over Peterson's place out on Route 65, Lombardi's gambling, and Pratt's union connections. Everything else he'll farm out. He'll get a piece of every racket left in town."

"And what will your boss have to say about this?"

"Doesn't matter, it's a done deal. There will always be people who want to gamble, or who need something the Law won't allow them to have. That means there will always be crime, and someone to control it. I'd rather it be controlled by only one man, rather than competing bosses."

"And that man's my father?" There was more than one question in those five words.

"And that man's your father." Devlin sat up, and acknowledged all her questions with another hug.

"And what about us, when the Commissioner sends you after him?"

"The courts, City Hall and the D.A.'s office are all clean, or as clean as they can get. Your father's working without a net. If he falls, it will be from carelessness, and the Commissioner won't need me to bring him in." After a pause he added, "Your father is not a careless man."

"I won't betray my father."

"I'll never ask you to. The rest we leave until tomorrow, or the next day."

"Or whenever."

"Agreed."

"Frank, what about tomorrow, the real tomorrow, I mean?"

"I report back to work, and then . . ."

"Then what?"

"I go on a wolf hunt. But not," Devlin gave her a smile, "Until tomorrow."

Angela smiled back. "Tomorrow," she said, and let the sheet fall.

Chapter Seven
Devil's End

The morning following the massacre at Dave's Place, the press besieged police headquarters. They wanted to know about the scores of dead that had been taken from there to the morgue, and why the few wounded taken to area hospitals were being held under heavy guard, with police physicians being brought in to treat them. There was a rumor that the Police Commissioner himself had received a gunshot wound, and the press wanted to know if it was true.

The reporters demanded to know what had happened. Who had started the battle inside the notorious gangland bar and who had been involved? They wanted to know how many of the victims were police, and how many were gang members. Word from the morgue was that two of the underworld's biggest bosses were among the dead, as were several of their lieutenants. Was this true, and if so, did this mean the start of another gang war in Harbor City. And, as always, they wanted to know about the Devil.

Detective Sergeant Frank Devlin was still officially missing and presumed dead. Work crews were still clearing away the rubble of the Fremont Tower, and counting the bodies that came out of it. So far, none had been identified as that of Sergeant Devlin.

One rumor that had come out of the massacre concerned the Devil's involvement. His name had been on the lips of several of the wounded men. A few were heard begging to be saved from the fires of Hell. The ambulance attendants anxiously passed this news to those reporters willing to pay for it.

The Police Commissioner, walking unaided although with a limp that did not escape notice, was surrounded by the press as he left his car and entered police headquarters. He had no comment.

Neither did Anton Szold, the head of Harbor City's Internal Affairs Division, who arrived shortly after the Commissioner. Shortly after their arrival, a police spokesman promised a statement later that afternoon. Until then, the reporters would have to wait.

"Well, what are we going to tell them?" The Commissioner asked the other two men in his office.

"Why not tell them the truth?" snapped Szold. "Tell the press that you, Sergeant Campbell here, and that private investigator you hired found out about a party being thrown to celebrate the end of the Devil. Tell them how you three went to the bar to avenge his death. Then tell them how just before you were about to do something stupid like trying to arrest a room full of armed and drunken men, you were saved by Sergeant Devlin's return from the grave. Finally, tell them that Sergeant Devlin, the Devil, your handpicked special agent assigned to bring justice back to this gang-ridden town, machine-gunned a room full of people without giving them a chance to surrender."

"That's not exactly how it happened, Mr. Szold."

"No, Sergeant Campbell?" Szold turned toward the detective. He was all too familiar with how police officers covered and explained away each other's actions. He was anxious to hear how Sergeant Campbell would rationalize the killing of so many people.

"Tell me then, Sergeant, what did I leave out?"

Campbell met the IAD man's eye. Whatever he believed Devlin had done, he wasn't going to let this man have him. "With respect, sir, you left out the part about Sergeant Devlin not firing until more than one of those in the bar had pulled out their guns. As I see it, he acted in self defense, and it was just luck or providence that had caused him to bring that Tommy gun with him."

Szold turned his attention back to the Commissioner. "Was that how it happened, or would Devlin had opened fire on those men anyway?"

The Commissioner put his hands together on his desk. He thought a moment, then answered his chief of Internal Affairs. "We all have our suspicions, Anton, but that's all they are, suspicions. Whatever his original intentions, Sergeant Devlin did wait until there were guns drawn on him. If that answer doesn't satisfy you, you are, of course, free to conduct your own investigation and bring whatever charges you think necessary." Both men knew that, without independent witnesses, any investigation would be fruitless and any charges brought could not be sustained.

The Commissioner stood up and extended his hand to Szold, a polite dismissal. "Now if you'll excuse us, Anton, Sergeant Campbell and I have some things to discuss."

Szold took the offered hand. He knew when to pull back and he had the patience to wait for a better time. For now, Devlin was the Commissioner's problem. If it wasn't solved this time, Szold would have another chance. "This is not over, Commissioner. What was once a good idea is now out of control. Do something now, before the Devil has to choose between you and his girlfriend." With this warning he left the room.

After Szold had left, Campbell waited a moment then went to the door. He opened it, and checked the hallway. It was empty.

"It's okay to talk, he's gone."

"He would be, Sergeant. Listening at doors is not Mr. Szold's style."

Campbell sat back down. "No? I thought that was in the IAD job description." When his chief didn't respond to his jibe Campbell went on. "He was right though. Devlin had been trapped, ambushed, and blown up. They were celebrating his death. He brought that machine gun to the party for a reason, and he was going to use it, good reason or no."

"I wish that I could say that I thought you were wrong, Sergeant. Or that you were right. The hell of it is, I just don't know."

"Well, sir, maybe when Devlin reports back to work he'll clear things up."

There was a false hope in Campbell's voice and both men knew it. Devlin's return would only make matters worse. What was to be done with a cop whom you suspected of being capable of slaughtering a roomful of people?

Both men sat for a while, worrying about that unspoken question. An officer of the law had to be trusted to follow that law, to give every citizen the protection that the law provided. He definitely should not use deadly force against a citizen except to protect his own life or the lives of others. Up until last night, Devlin had been very careful to follow that rule. Last night, he had come very close to breaking it. True, last night his targets had been criminals, many of them mobsmen who deserved death a dozen times. The others present had all been accessories either before or after the fact to the crimes that had held Harbor City hostage for so long.

But that was last night. Devlin, for all his bravery and skill, was still just a man, and men make mistakes. What if the next time the Devil decided to be judge, jury, and executioner, his targets included innocent people? That was a chance that the Commissioner could not take, and both men knew it.

Campbell was the first to break the silence.

"What did Mr. Szold mean about Devlin choosing between you and his girlfriend?"

The Commissioner let out a sigh. "For some time now, Sergeant Devlin has been involved with Angela Martinelli."

Campbell was stunned. "Sir, please tell me that's it's an Angela Martinelli different from the one who's the daughter of Harbor City's only surviving mob boss."

The Commissioner's silence and pained expression was Campbell's answer. The sergeant let out a long, slow whistle. "We do have a problem."

"Two problems, Sergeant. The first is what to tell the press about last night."

In the end, they decided to tell the truth, most of it anyway. A spokesman told the press that the investigation into the bombing of the Fremont Tower had lead police to Dave's Place. Once there, one of the officers was recognized, and a gunfight broke out. A number of Harbor City's more prominent gangsters had been killed, with only minor casualties on the part of the police. He did not take questions. No mention was made of the Devil, leaving the press to speculate as they would.

While the press was getting an abbreviated version of the truth, Sergeant Frank Devlin returned home for the first time in several days. Since escaping from the wreckage that had been the Fremont Tower, he had spent his time recovering from the injuries he had received and planning his wake with Angela's father. Just as he had been led into a trap, so he had laid one for those he was sworn to bring to justice. Months ago, the Commissioner had told to him to end Harbor City's gang problem by any means necessary. By night's end, with the cream of Harbor City's underworld lying dead or seriously wounded, the problem had been solved.

Devlin was not too worried about Louis Martinelli, the city's one remaining gang boss. Martinelli would be too busy consolidating his power to cause the city much trouble. He would also have to do it without his usual support base. Michael Shaw, a special agent brought in by the Commissioner, had rooted out and cleaned up the corruption that had pervaded the courts and City Hall. Martinelli no doubt still had a few contacts that would prove useful, but for the most part, and for the first time in many years, Harbor City had an honest government. It was hard to see how crime could flourish in such unfertile ground.

"The gangs are beaten, the city's honest, so is the Devil still needed?"

Angela had asked him this just before they had parted earlier that morning. He had been wondering that himself, and the question was on his mind as he let himself into his apartment.

He had no sooner closed the door behind him when he realized he was not alone. He looked over the living room carefully, his eyes finally settling on a corner not touched by the afternoon sun. To the shadows he said, "You can come out now, Mr. Shaw."

Shaw stood up and walked toward Devlin. "After last night you should call me Michael."

With his right arm in a sling, a result from the previous night's shoot-out, Shaw offered his left hand in greeting. Devlin took it with a smile, more amused than upset about this invasion of his home.

"Michael it is, and it's Frank to you."

"What gave me away? I used to be fairly good at this."

Devlin pointed to Shaw's injured arm. "The antiseptic the hospital used. You've had time to get used to the smell. It hit me as soon as I came in."

Devlin walked into the kitchen. "Coffee?" Shaw nodded and sat himself at the kitchen table while Devlin brewed a pot.

As the coffee was brewing, Devlin asked after the Commissioner and Sergeant Campbell. Shaw told him that both men had been injured, but neither seriously.

Devlin handed Shaw his cup and sat across from him. "You're here about Hopkins."

Shaw nodded, "Among other things."

"He survived last night, then?"

"He was never there, Frank. Hopkins was never one to celebrate with a crowd, and he's smart enough to have anticipated the presence of the police seeking vengeance for one of their own."

"Does he know that I'm still alive?"

"No one does, except for the four of us, and anyone you've told."

"His employers are dead, what's he likely to do once he finds out I made it out of the building?"

"He'll keep trying to kill you. Hopkins considers himself a man of his word. He took money to kill you, and he'll keep his end of the bargain. Besides, by killing you, he'll make himself a name in this town. That will help if he wants to form a gang. Finally, he will come after you if for no other reason than he'll be expecting you to come after him."

Devlin thought about this, took a sip of coffee, and said, "He's right to do so. I will be going after him. After all, if you let one crook drop a building on you, pretty soon they'll all want to do it. The only question is, how do I find him first?"

"That shouldn't be too hard, Frank. Think, by now he's heard rumors that you're still alive, but there's been no confirmation. If you were in his place, where would you be looking?"

"If he knew where I lived, he'd come here first, but like most Harbor City cops, my phone's unlisted and I'm not listed in any city directory."

"Smart move," said Shaw. "And Hopkins hasn't had time to make the contacts to get your address from police records. Still, there are other places he could try."

"The police station for one place," Shaw nodded agreement. "The morgue, hospitals . . ."

"And ..." prompted Shaw.

"And ... ah!"

"Exactly," said Shaw as Devlin realized what he had been suggesting.

"Good idea, Michael, I'll go there first thing tomorrow morning."

Would you like some help?"

"Thanks, but I'll make my own arrangements."

Devlin stood up and walked over to the coffeepot.

"Let me heat that up for you, Michael, and you can tell me your other reasons for coming over."

"Well, to start with, how did you get out of that building?"

Nine o'clock the next morning found Devlin at the site of what had been the Fremont Tower. The clean-up crew had arrived, but had not yet begun work. The heavy bulldozers, backhoes, and cranes were silent; after all, there were still coffee and doughnuts to be eaten, and last night's prizefight had yet to be re-fought. Finally, at a signal audible only to them, the men tossed out the last of the coffee, wadded up the cups and threw them in the general direction of the trashcans. Some of the cups actually made it in.

As the big machines were being fired up, Devlin looked around. There were the usual onlookers for a site like this, retired men with nothing better to do, jobless men who should have been at the foreman's shack asking for day labor, and young boys who should have been at school. There was a detail from the City Morgue, waiting for more bodies to be recovered. A photographer from the Crime Lab was there, to snap a final picture of the deceased. Members of the press were there with their cameras as well, hoping that someone famous, or at least notorious, would be uncovered.

"If they're hoping to find me," Devlin said to himself, "They'll be disappointed." Devlin resisted the temptation to walk up to one of the reporters detailed to the site and ask if he had been found yet. His survival was still officially a secret, known only to a few in the department, Angela and her father, and those who had survived Dave's Place. For that reason he kept his hat pulled over his eyes and hung back in the shadows of nearby buildings.

It was eleven thirty when a police whistle blew, stopping work. A man who had been carefully working alongside a crane pulling debris from the center of the site was waving a bright yellow flag he had pulled from his pocket. The coroner's men and the police photographer put on their hard hats and walked over to the crane.

The crime lab man stopped short of where the discovery had been made and took a picture of the general area. He then joined the others and took a picture of the body that had been found.

This was what Devlin had been waiting for. Idly wondering which of the many men he had killed that day it was, he watched as the corpse was put into a body bag and zippered shut.

As the men made their stumbling way back to their wagon, Devlin shifted his attention to the crowd nearest it. As he expected, a reasonably well dressed man separated from the crowd and slowly made his way over to the morgue truck, timing his movements to arrive just as the men from the morgue got there with their burden.

The man wasn't from the newspapers. The Press didn't pay for information it would get later that day for free. He wasn't a cop. Except for the man from the Lab, none had been assigned to this detail. It had to be the man he was looking for.

Even from a distance Devlin recognized the man. He was

Mitch Barrow, formerly a soldier with the Peterson gang. His boss was dead, killed by Wolf Hopkins and used as a final piece of bait in Hopkins's trap for the Devil. Devlin wondered if Barrow knew his boss was dead, and, if so, who had killed him. He also wondered if Barrow would care if he did know.

The corpse was laid on a waiting gurney. However, before it was slid into the truck, Barrow walked over to the attendants, who acted as if they expected him. An envelope changed hands, and the body bag was unzipped. Barrow compared the corpse with a photo he had taken from his pocket, shook his head, and walked back into the crowd.

Just at noon, at another unheard signal, the workers broke for lunch. Barrow got into his car and drove away. Devlin followed in his own car and was lead to the Armistead Hotel.

Devlin parked on the street behind Barrow, but allowed him to cross over to the hotel before he got out of his car. Devlin looked around. There was a park across the street. That would do. Satisfied, Devlin went home.

The next morning, Devlin stationed himself in the park. He had dressed himself as a man who had been out of work for some time, a man who had despaired of ever finding a job and who was now content to waste his day on a park bench. There were enough of these men in Harbor City that one more would not be noticed. A bottle by his side added to his illusion of idleness. The paper bag wrapped around the bottle kept anyone from seeing that it was empty.

From his bench, Devlin watched the coming and goings at the hotel. He saw Barrow leave, no doubt returning to the ruins of the hotel to resume his useless wait for the Devil's exhumation.

There was no point in following Barrow, so Devlin continued to wait and watch. By noon, he had seen several men whom he recognized as having belonged to one gang or the other go into the Armistead. Some of these men came out quickly, anger or disappointment on their faces. Others took longer to emerge. When they did, their faces bore the relieved looks of men who had just found new jobs after suddenly losing their old ones. It seemed to Devlin that Hopkins was recruiting a new pack, and being choosy in whom he picked.

Devlin wondered how the word had spread so fast. A week ago, Hopkins was a stranger to Harbor City. Now, every gangster left alive not only knew where he lived but was trying to hook on with him. Devlin's question was answered when he saw Alan Morse come out of the hotel.

Alan Morse! I thought that weasel had left town after I roughed him up in the alley. Devlin thought back to the night he had brought down Tom Woods and Eddie Frazier in Lombardi's casino. Morse had left town that night, afraid of what might happen to him for ratting out his friends. No matter that the Devil had beaten the information out of him. Morse's boss, Enoch Kruger, would have Morse killed for his betrayal, and Morse knew it.

Devlin recalled that Morse had left for New York before waiting to see the results of his forced conversation with the Devil. So he didn't know that after the Devil had killed Frazier and put Woods in the hospital, he had gone on to kill Kruger. If he learned of Kruger's death later, he didn't bother to return. While in New York, Morse had obviously come to the notice of Hopkins. Hopkins must have brought the man down to assist him in the recruiting of local talent.

This was not good. Hopkins was forming a gang, which meant that he planned on staying in Harbor City for awhile. And unlike the criminal organizations of Lombardi, Pratt and Martinelli, this gang would deal in robbery, murder, and mayhem on a public scale. If he were allowed to succeed, Hopkins would subject Harbor City to a new round of terror. He had to be stopped, and quickly.

Devlin stood up. He upended his bottle as if to be sure that he had drained its last drop. Appearing disgusted and still thirsty, he threw it in a nearby trashcan. Then he left the park walking east, and followed Alan Morse home.

Devlin's next move came two days later, after the steady

stream of gunmen at the Armistead Hotel had stopped. That day, Devlin wandered over to the site of the Fremont. Barrow was still standing his lonely vigil, waiting for but no longer expecting Devlin's body to be found. Again, Devlin followed him after the work crews had quit for the day. This time he was led to the Hotel Belvedere. As expected, Hopkins had relocated after forming his gang.

That night, Alan Morse was dreaming the dreams of the unjust, of rolling sevens with two girls at his side when his bedroom door burst open. A hooded man came through the door. Before Morse could react, he was pulled out of bed and thrown against a wall. He was then picked off the floor and lashed to a chair. A shade was taken of a table lamp and put on the nightstand next to him. The light was turned on, blinding him. The man stayed in the shadows.

"I need to know what Hopkins's next move is, Alan," said a voice somewhat familiar to Morse. "We can do this easy or hard."

Morse's answer was short and four-lettered. A fist came out if the darkness and hit Morse in the stomach. A hand slapped his face.

"Tell me what Hopkins is planning, Alan, what's the job?"

"Look, whoever you are, Hopkins is nobody to fool with. He brought down the Devil, and he'll take care of you too."

A short laugh came out of the shadows. The light was moved away from Morse's face to brighten the room. Morse's eyes adjusted. The man in the hood took off his mask.

"So I'm dead, am I, Alan? Want to join me?"

Morse refused to believe what his eyes told him. The Devil was dead, Hopkins had assured him, his body buried under the rubble of the Fremont. The man who had machine-gunned Dave's Place had been a police plant. "No," was all he managed to utter in denial of his senses.

The Devil put his face up close to Morse's. "Yes, Alan, it's me. And if you think that you're not going to tell me what I need to know, remember what I did to you in that alley. Remember what I did to Frazier and Woods. Remember Johnson, Tomas, and

Kruger. Remember the dead of Dave's Place. They're all in Hell, Alan, and I hear their voices. Every night they cry to me in my sleep, 'Send more souls.' I need a reason not to send them yours, Alan." Devlin reached into his pocket and took out a switchblade knife. He flicked it open before Morse's eyes. "Do you want to join them, Alan, one piece at a time?"

Morse began shaking his head back and forth, his eyes never leaving the knife blade before him. "No, no, no, no ..." he kept repeating.

"Then tell me, Alan, what's the job. Hopkins has to have a job planned, to test his men, to keep them happy. Tell me, Alan." The Devil gently ran the knife along the top of Morse's left ear, not hard enough to break the skin, but enough for Morse to feel the blade. "Tell me, Alan, what's the job?"

Morse broke. "The Harbor City Trust. Tonight. They're breaking in and blowing the safe."

"Will Hopkins be with them?"

"No, he said that that this was 'an audition.' If they pull it off, they're in his gang. If not, he'd look elsewhere."

"He's going to have to look elsewhere, then." The Devil shoved a gag in Morse's mouth.

"Don't worry, Alan, if I live through the night, I'll call the cops and tell them where to find you. If not, well, I'll apologize when we meet in Hell."

Devlin went down to the street and got into his car. As he drove to the Trust Company he planned his next moves. There were at least a half dozen men in Hopkins's gang, maybe more. Devlin was fully armed - three guns, two knives and a shotgun in the trunk. The gang would be in the bank by now. He'd wait for them to come out, and pick them off one by one. Those that retreated into the bank, he'd go after and hunt down. By morning, Hopkins's new gang would all be dead.

No! Devlin started shaking and pulled the car over to avoid a crash. *What am I doing, he asked himself. My blood is racing, my pulse pounding. My God! I've come to enjoy this.* A wave of nausea hit him. He opened the car door and was sick on the street. When he recovered, he realized that Frank Devlin might have gone into the Fremont Tower, but only the Devil had come out. *How many more men will I have to kill?* He thought back to Alan Morse, how he had tortured the man for information the Devil needed. He had felt a perverse satisfaction when Morse broke, when he had betrayed Hopkins. He remembered smiling as he left Morse bound and alone in his room, left him to die if the Devil fell tonight.

There had been no such feeling the first time he had beaten Morse outside Lombardi's or when he had terrorized the maitre d' of the Shot Tower. At the time, those incidents had just been nasty jobs that had needed to be done. Or so he told himself.

What have I become? Devlin knew the answer. For far too long, he had been two people. He needed to become one again.

Devlin got out of his car and found a pay phone. He called the Commissioner at home and told him of the planned robbery at the Trust Company. He told him about Alan Morse, and where to find the man. Devlin hung up the phone. There was just one job left before he could let the Devil go. He got back into his car and drove home to Angela.

The next morning, Devlin was waiting in the lobby of The Belvedere when Barrow came down from his room. Devlin stopped him before he could get to the street.

"Hey, buddy, let go!" The man yelled as Devlin grabbed his arm to keep him from going through the revolving doors. He looked over to the hotel detective, who was very noticeably not paying any attention. Devlin had already shown the security man his badge and warned him off.

Barrow tried to pull away and Devlin's grip tightened.

"Go back upstairs," Devlin told the man, "And tell your new boss that his search is over. Tell him I'll be in the park down the street, waiting for him."

Being a native of Harbor City, and having looked at his photograph several times over the past few days, Barrow should have recognized Devlin. Still, real life is different, and he was expecting to find Devlin dead, not standing in some lobby with a vise grip on his arm.

"Right, like my boss would want to see you. Why should he care what you've got to say?"

Devlin ignored the question. He let go of Barrow's arm and instead took hold of his shirt at the collar. Twisting, Devlin shut off most of the man's air. He pulled Barrow close and let the man struggle for breath for a few seconds. Finally he whispered, "Tell Hopkins it's time to pay for his sins."

He pushed Barrow away, relaxing his grip at the same time. The man fell over the back of a couch. He got to his feet in time to see Devlin walk past the front windows on his way to the park. The Devil stopped and glared at him through the glass, delivering a final, unspoken message.

Barrow turned and ran for the stairs, tripping up them in his haste to deliver the Devil's message. As he ran up the steps, he decided that it was time to leave Harbor City as quickly as possible. He had no desire to be anywhere around if the Devil, dead or alive, came back again to haunt him.

The entrance to the park was at an angle to the street corner. Devlin walked through the stone archway and selected the third bench on the right, one fully shaded by a large oak just behind the bench. There, with his back to the tree, he sat down to wait.

He did not have to wait long. About fifteen minutes after he had sent the gasping Barrows off to fetch Hopkins, the man he was after calmly walked into the park. Hopkins stopped a minute beneath the archway and looked around. He smiled slightly as he recognized Devlin, as if happy to see an old friend. Without a greeting he sat down next to the detective.

"You went down the dumbwaiter and out through the subway extension, didn't you?"

Devlin hated this part. He was going to sit here and make polite conversation with the man who had tried to kill him. He did not want to do it, but it was necessary. He had to finish this, to put this part of his life behind him and begin the next.

Devlin did not bother to face Hopkins. Instead, he kept his gaze fixed on a distance part of the park. "Does it matter?" he asked.

"No, I suppose not. Still, it would be nice to know I guessed correctly."

Devlin now turned toward Hopkins. "I guess you'll have to go to your grave wondering."

"Is that a threat, Devlin? Are there men lurking behind the tress waiting to shoot me down."

"No, Hopkins, there are no men out there, unless you've stationed some, and I don't think you had enough time to do that." Devlin turned and faced the park again. "No, I just asked you out here to talk."

"About what?"

Devlin shifted so that his whole body was now facing Hopkins. "I'm tired, Hopkins. I'm tired of this game of cops and robbers, tired of being the Devil. I'm tired of people trying to kill me and of my having to shoot them before they do."

Hopkins was clearly amazed at this honesty. During his rise in New York's underworld, he had become a very good judge of people and character. Devlin was not just feeding him a line. He was tired. Hopkins could read that in his face. He wanted to quit. Maybe Devlin had survived the bombing of the Fremont Towers, but the Devil was almost finished.

"How does this concern me, Devlin?"

"You're a dangerous man, Hopkins. I've read the reports about you from New York – a gang leader who went to prison. When you got out it was more of the same – robbery, extortion, kidnappings, murder. You do it all, for yourself and for hire. You're a natural predator. I can't leave Harbor City with you running loose. I can't stay here either, not without having to worry about when you're going to try to kill me again."

Devlin's voice went up as he finished his sentence, turning it into a question. Hopkins pursed his lips, as if thinking over his answer. Then he gave Devlin a small smile, and nodded his head.

That was all the answer the Devil needed.

"Then again, Hopkins, you can't operate in this city without worrying about when I'm going to come after you."

"Are you suggesting something, Devlin? If so, make it clear."

"Leave town. Go back to New York. If you do, I'll forget what happened at the Fremont."

"New York, Detective Devlin, was becoming uncomfortable for me. There was a certain Mr. Shaw who was starting to investigate my activities. Besides, I like it here." This time Hopkins turned away and looked into the park.

Devlin sat back, disappointed. "Then you leave me no choice, Hopkins."

"You have no choice, Devlin. You want to arrest me, I surrender." Hopkins held out his wrists for handcuffs. "There are no charges you can hold me on. You have no evidence that I committed any crime in this city."

"Half the crooks arrested at the Harbor City Trust Company last night named you as their leader."

"And I'm sure the other half swore that I had nothing to do with that. Have you any real evidence?"

Devlin tried again. "I have a paper in your handwriting taken from the dead body of Tony Peterson."

"Produce the body. Produce the weapon that killed him and tie me to it. Prove I was anywhere near wherever it was you found his body. You do that, and I'll confess to whatever you like."

"You don't understand do you? I'm giving you one last chance."

"Or what, you'll kill me? One thing I do know about you is that you won't do that unless I'm foolish enough to pull a gun on you. That I won't do. Whatever happens, you won't see it coming."

"I know, Hopkins, I know."

Devlin stood up, turned and offered Hopkins his hand. "Well, you can't say I didn't try."

Surprised, Hopkins also stood and shook with the detective. "You did at that, Devlin, you at that. May the best of us win."

The Devil dropped his hand to his side. "I'm sorry, Hopkins,

I really am."

Too late Hopkins realized that the handshake had been a signal. He heard the muffled report of a rifle. A moment later, a high velocity bullet went through his head and into the tree behind him.

Hopkins had been eye to eye with Devlin up until the end. In his last second, he looked for some sign of victory to cross the Devil's face. He found none, only regret and pity.

Devlin watched the body fall. "I'm sorry," he said again, then turned and walked out of the park.

Devlin waited until the lunch rush was over, then picked Angela up at her father's restaurant. The two went for a walk through Little Italy.

"Nice shooting this morning," he finally said, after the two had walked for awhile.

"Thank my father, he taught me how to use a gun."

"Angela, I . . . "

"Don't start again, Dev. We talked about this last night. I had to do it; there was no one else to ask. Certainly not anyone in the police department, and you couldn't trust Shaw not to shoot if you didn't give the signal. My father's people, no, you couldn't trust them either. They would have used it against you sooner or later."

"I should have done it myself."

"Which is what Hopkins was waiting for. You make a move, he makes a move. Maybe you're faster, maybe he is. Fifty-fifty, Dev. This way was a sure thing."

Angela stopped walking. Her one arm around him already, she turned toward him and hugged him tight.

"Besides, if we're going to be partners, I'll have to do my share of the work, and you'll have to let me."

"Then you've decided?"

"Yes, and yes again, to both your questions."

It was the first good news Devlin had heard all week.

"You're sure about this, son?"

"Yes sir, as sure as I was when I first picked up that badge."

Devlin and the Commissioner both looked down on the desk at the gold badge and service revolver lying on its surface. Devlin had handed them to the Commissioner just moments before along with his letter of resignation.

"What will you do now, Frank?" asked Sergeant Campbell. The sergeant had been in the Commissioner's office when Devlin came in, and Devlin had asked him to stay.

"Michael Shaw has offered us jobs with his organization. We've decided to accept."

"Us, we?" Campbell wasn't sure who was being talking about, and was half-afraid that Devlin meant to include him, or worse, that Devlin had started thinking of the Devil as a separate person.

"Myself and Angela, Ben."

"You'll be working with that mobster's daughter, then?"

"No, Ben, I'll be working with my wife."

Campbell wisely decided to let the matter drop as the Commissioner extended his hand.

"Well, congratulations, Frank. When's the wedding?"

"In a week or to, we've still some arrangements to make. I hope you'll both be able to make it. I could use a couple of best men."

All three men knew what Devlin was asking. For the Police Commissioner and his top homicide investigator to attend the wedding of a gangland princess was politically not a good idea. If the papers found out they would make it the scandal of the year.

"Politics be damned, son, of course we'll be there. Right, Benjamin?"

"We've been through Hell together. Just try and keep me away."

Devlin smiled, "Then that's settled. I don't think we'll be having a big ceremony anyway. Neither we nor her father want to draw attention to ourselves right now. He never was one for publicity, and right now most people think I'm dead. It's probably best I stay that way."

"Understandable, Frank," agreed the Commissioner. "I'm already hearing talk that it was your ghost that came back and shot up Dave's Place. We'll let rumors like that build, refuse to comment on any questions about your demise or survival, and let fear and superstition do some of our work for us."

"And if you ever do need me, contact Shaw. If I can I'll be back, and the Devil's ghost will haunt Harbor City once more."

JOHN L. FRENCH has worked for over thirty-five years
as a crime scene investigator and has seen more than his share
of murders, shootings, and serious assaults. As a break from
the realities of his job, he writes science fiction, pulp, horror,
fantasy, and, of course, crime fiction.

In 1992 John began writing stories based on his training
and experiences on the streets of Baltimore. His first story "Past
Sins" was published in Hardboiled Magazine and was cited as
one of the best Hardboiled stories of 1993. More crime fiction
followed, appearing in Alfred Hitchcock's Mystery Magazine,
the Fading Shadows magazines and in collections by Barnes
and Noble. Association with writers like James Chambers and
the late, great C.J. Henderson led him to try horror fiction and
to a still growing fascination with zombies and other undead
things. His first horror story "The Right Solution" appeared in
Marietta Publishing's Lin Carter's Anton Zarnak. Other horror
stories followed in anthologies such as The Dead Walk and
Dark Furies, both published by Die Monster Die books. It was
in Dark Furies that Bianca Jones made her literary debut in "21
Doors," a story based on an old Baltimore legend and a creepy
game his daughter used to play with her friends.

John's first book was The Devil of Harbor City, a novel done
in the old pulp style. Past Sins and Here There Be Monsters
soon followed. John was also consulting editor for Chelsea
House's Criminal Investigation series. His other books include
The Assassins' Ball (Written with Patrick Thomas), Paradise
Denied, Blood Is the Life and The Nightmare Strikes. John is the
editor of To Hell In A Fast Car, Mermaids 13, C. J. Henderson's
Challenge of the Unknown, and (with Greg Schauer) With
Great Power…

MURPHY'S LORE

Help is only a Rainbow *Away*...

"Mix Gaiman's American Gods and Robinson's Callahan's Crosstime Saloon on Prachett's Discworld and you get an idea of Thomas' Murphy's Lore." -David Sherman, author of STARFIST and Demontech

MAIREANN DÓCHAS IS GLIODAR
I Followed the Rainbow to Bulfinche's Pub
NEW YORK EST. 1886
MURPHYS-LORE.COM

"ENTERTAINING, INVENTIVE AND DELIGHTFULLY CREEPY." -JONATHAN MABERRY, New York Times and Bram Stoker Award Winning Author

"SLICK... ENTERTAINING Paul Di Filippo, ASIMOV'S

"HUMOR, OUTRAGEOUS ADVENTURES, & SOME CLEVER PLOT TWISTS." -Don D'Ammassa, SCIENCE FICTION CHRONICLE

PATRICK THOMAS

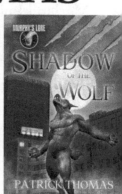

"Patrick Thomas is... so believable it's unbelievable."
-Ida Vega-Landow, The Journal of the Lincoln Heights Literary Society

DEAD TO RITES
Patrick Thomas
C.J. Henderson

rites of Passage
John L. French
Patrick Thomas

When Darkness Falls
The Department of
Mystic Affairs
Picks up the pieces

From The Murphy's Lore Universe of
PATRICK THOMAS
www.patthomas.net

Find us on Facebook!

Even the things that go **Bump** in the night
will learn that you __DON'T__ mess with...
Terrorbelle

Fairy Rides the Lightning
PATRICK THOMAS

Fairy With A Gun
PATRICK THOMAS

"Thomas certainly brings the goods to the table
when it comes to writing urban fiction...I promise, you will love...
Terrorbelle: Fairy With a Gun. Who doesn't love a well-stacked,
ass-kicking, gun-toting, woman with bullet-proof, razor-sharp win
that investigates all manner of supernatural spookiness? I know
and Thomas's humor shows through in every tale. Jim Butcher ar
Laurell K Hamilton have nothing on Thomas." The Raven's Barro

More

TerrorBelle
the Unconquered

From the heart of Murphy's Lore

PATRICK THOMAS

From The Murph   re Universe of
PA   THOMA

hape up...
You only get
NE Warning

Hell's
Detective

No One Is Above The **Lore**...
Even In Hell

Invocation
PATRICK THOMAS

Darkness CURSED
Hex
PATRICK THOMAS

LORE & DYSORDER
PATRICK THOMAS

SHADOWS
PATRICK THOMAS
JOHN L. FRENCH

CASE
MOON MANIAC

"Dark... and charming."
- Ellen Datlow,
The Best Horror of the Year Vol. 4

IT'S A CRIME
TO MISS THESE
GREAT STORIES!

from author
John L. French

WWW.PADWOLF.COM

You can't get better than 13!

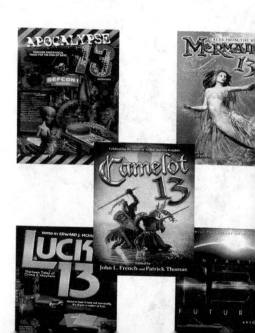

A detective's work is never done.
And don't call him Baby Bear...

NO TEACHERS.
NO PARENTS
CHOOL IS OUT....
OF THIS WORLD

KEEP THE DEAD out of our School

DOWN WI THI ZOM

HOME

The zombie apocalypse is over...

Now even undead kids have to go to school

15th Aniversary
Omnibus of
Books 1-6

5 SILLY MONSTERS JUMPING ON THE ZED

a picture book
for kids

DOWN THESE
MEANS STREETS
of Magic & Monsters walk the

MYSTIC INVESTIGATORS

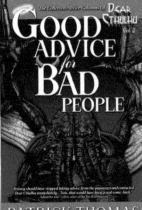

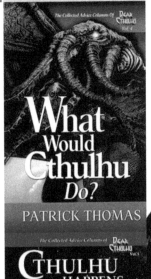

DEAR CTHULHU

The advice column to END all advice columns

WWW.DEARCTHULHU.COM
WWW.PADWOLF.COM

CPSIA information can be obtained
at www.ICGtesting.com
Printed in the USA
BVHW061742110222
628346BV00003B/18